Quiz no. 31538

Points 5.0

Ryan and Anna walked up
to Joe and David.

"You've done a nice job on this newsletter," Ryan said. "One of you must have a really great desktop-publishing program."

"I do," David said.

"Lucky you," Anna said. She wasn't smiling. "Are you going to publish *The Champ* every week? That's what we've been doing with *Sports Report*. It's a lot of work to publish it so often. But we think it's important."

Joe looked at David. "I guess . . . We haven't even talked about that."

Anna shrugged. "Maybe you haven't decided yet whether you want to take over the newsletter project completely. Maybe you just wanted to show up some eighth-graders."

"But—" David began.

The school bell rang just as David started to speak. Anna and Ryan turned away without saying another word. They entered the building. Everyone else followed them. The heavy double doors slammed shut.

The Adventures of **wishbone**™
titles in Large-Print Editions:

The Adventures of WISHBONE™

A Pup in King Arthur's Court

by **Joanne Barkan**
Inspired by *A Connecticut Yankee in King Arthur's Court*
by Mark Twain

WISHBONE™ created by Rick Duffield

Gareth Stevens Publishing
MILWAUKEE

This book is a work of fiction. The characters, incidents, and dialogues are products of the author's imagination and are not to be construed as real. Any resemblance to actual events or persons, living or dead, is entirely coincidental.

For a free color catalog describing Gareth Stevens' list of high-quality books and multimedia programs, call 1-800-542-2595 (USA) or 1-800-461-9120 (Canada). Gareth Stevens Publishing's Fax: (414) 225-0377.

Library of Congress Cataloging-in-Publication Data

Barkan, Joanne.
    A pup in King Arthur's Court / by Joanne Barkan; [interior illustrations by Arvis Stewart].
        p. cm.
    Originally published: Allen, Texas; Big Red Chair Books, © 1998.
(The adventures of Wishbone; #15)
        Summary: When Joe and David decide to use a computer to publish a sports newsletter that will outshine the one that the school produces, Wishbone is reminded of Mark Twain's story and imagines himself as Hank Morgan, a nineteenth-century American who travels back in time to King Arthur's court.
    ISBN 0-8368-2593-4 (lib. bdg.)
    [1. Dogs—Fiction. 2. Arthur, King—Fiction. 3. Knights and knighthood—Fiction. 4. Time travel—Fiction.] I. Stewart, Arvis L., ill. II. Title. III. Adventures of Wishbone; #15.
PZ7.B25039Pu   2000
[Fic]—dc21   99-051789

431 Gumdrop 3/01 13.30 F Wi

This edition first published in 2000 by
Gareth Stevens Publishing
1555 North RiverCenter Drive, Suite 201
Milwaukee, Wisconsin 53212 USA

© 1998 Big Feats! Entertainment. First published by Big Red Chair Books™, a Division of Lyrick Publishing™, 300 E. Bethany Drive, Allen, Texas 75002.

Edited by Pam Pollack
Copy edited by Jonathon Brodman
Cover design by Lyle Miller
Interior illustrations by Arvis Stewart
Wishbone photograph by Carol Kaelson

WISHBONE, the Wishbone portrait, and the Big Feats! Entertainment logo are trademarks and service marks of Big Feats! Entertainment.

Printed in the United States of America

1 2 3 4 5 6 7 8 9 04 03 02 01 00

*To my godson Russell Forbes Jensen
and his close relations (my dear friends):*

Forbesy Russell

Dennis Jensen

Betty Russell

Bob Russell

FROM THE BIG RED CHAIR . . .

Oh . . . hi! Wishbone here. You caught me right in the middle of some of my favorite things—books. Let me welcome you to THE ADVENTURES OF WISHBONE. In each of these books, I have adventures with my friends in Oakdale and imagine myself as a character in one of the greatest stories of all time. This story takes place in the fall, when Joe is twelve and he and his friends are in the sixth grade—during the first season of my television show. In *A PUP IN KING ARTHUR'S COURT*, I imagine I'm Hank Morgan, a nineteenth-century businessperson transported back in time to sixth-century England. The story is inspired by Mark Twain's classic tale, *A CONNECTICUT YANKEE IN KING ARTHUR'S COURT*. It's a hilarious twist in a classic setting where almost anything can happen.

You're in for a real treat, so pull up a chair and a snack and sink your teeth into *A PUP IN KING ARTHUR'S COURT!*

Chapter One

Wishbone stood at the edge of the Sequoyah Middle School's soccer field. A shiver of excitement went through his white fur. It ran down his spine to the black patch on his back. His ears—one brown and the other white with brown spots—stood up straight. He wagged his tail faster and faster.

What a game! he thought. *Tie score and only twenty seconds left to play! Can Wishbone stand the tension? Ha! You bet I can! "Excitement" is my middle name.*

The Jack Russell terrier turned to look at the noisy fans who filled the bleachers just behind him. They were cheering wildly for the Sequoyah soccer team. The ball had just sailed out of bounds.

"Go, Sequoyah! You can do it! *Score!*" the fans shouted.

Yes! Wishbone thought. *They* can *do it. If they win this game against the Franklin School, they'll go on to the sixth-grade district playoffs. Go, Sequoyah!*

Wishbone turned back to the playing field. His eyes focused on one Sequoyah player—twelve-year-old Joe

Talbot. He and Wishbone lived together and were best friends. Despite the cool October air, Joe's straight brown hair was wet with perspiration.

That's my boy, Wishbone thought. *I've taught him everything he knows about playing ball—and he is gooood!* Wishbone barked. "Hey, Joe! Show 'em our stuff!"

A Franklin player went after the out-of-bounds ball and grabbed it. He paused a moment until one of his teammates was in a favorable position. Then he threw the ball back onto the field—in the direction of a Franklin midfielder.

Wishbone panted. "Living on the edge really works for me."

The Franklin midfielder started to dribble the ball up the field. His footwork was excellent. He dribbled with speed and control.

Wishbone nodded. "Not bad—especially for someone with just two feet."

Sequoyah's defense closed in fast. The Franklin midfielder glanced around to see which of his teammates was open to receive a pass. He kicked. The ball curved slightly too far to the right. Joe Talbot raced forward—and intercepted the pass.

Wishbone leaped into the air. "Way to go, Joe!"

The Sequoyah fans roared their approval. Their shouting turned into one strong voice. They stamped on the wood planks of the bleachers and made a sound like thunder.

For a moment, the field in front of Joe was wide open. He took off in a flash, dribbling downfield at top speed.

"Take it all the way!" the Sequoyah fans screamed.

Wishbone blocked out all the sounds around him.

He concentrated hard. He held his body so still that not even his whiskers moved. He kept his eyes glued on Joe and the ball. Time seemed to slow down for him. It was as if he were watching the last five seconds of the game in slow motion.

Joe was within scoring range. He stopped the ball with his right foot. He glanced at the goalie and aimed for the upper left corner of the goal. His right leg swung back. Franklin's star defense player charged in from the side. Joe kicked—a powerful high kick off the shoelaces— just as the Franklin player crashed into him. Both players went down. The ball flew over the goalie's outstretched arm. Goal!

The buzzer sounded. The crowd roared even louder. Wishbone threw his lean body into the air. He twisted into a flip, then landed neatly on all fours. He turned to look at Joe.

"That was gr——" Wishbone froze. He saw Joe sitting on the ground. The Franklin player who had run into Joe was sitting next to him. Both players were rubbing their heads.

The referee blew his whistle—two short blasts. All the other players immediately stopped moving and knelt on the field. They always did that when someone seemed to be injured. The two coaches and the referee ran over to Joe and the Franklin player.

Wishbone barked. "Joe, are you hurt? Well—there's only one way to find out."

Using his sturdy shoulders, Wishbone pushed between the legs of the people gathered at the edge of the field. A moment later, he was racing across the field.

"Hey! What's that dog doing?" someone shouted.

Wishbone's four legs moved even faster. *What am I*

doing? I'm Joe's personal healer—as well as his personal trainer. I take care of his legal business, too. So don't try any weird treatments until I arrive.

Wishbone slowed down as he came near the two boys and the adults bending over them. He squeezed between the legs of the referee and the Sequoyah coach.

"What's the dog doing here?" the referee asked.

"He belongs to Joe," the Sequoyah coach said.

Joe turned his head and saw Wishbone. He grinned and reached out to rub his pal between the ears.

"Don't worry, boy," Joe said. "It's just a bump on my head."

Wishbone noticed a lump on the right side of Joe's forehead. The Franklin player had the exact same kind of lump in the middle his forehead.

Wishbone breathed a sigh of relief. "Nothing serious. But let's begin treating these injuries right away. The best remedy is . . . a snack—for all of us. I usually prescribe pizza. Large size, extra sausage—"

"Let's get some ice packs on those foreheads," the Sequoyah coach said.

Wishbone barked. "Ice? Do you really think that's a nourishing thing to do?"

Joe and the Franklin player stood up.

Wishbone sighed. "Nobody ever listens to the dog."

As the group started to walk off the field, a big cheer went up from the bleachers. Joe's teammates ran over to him. The Sequoyah fans called out and waved to him. Joe smiled at the crowd and waved back.

"I guess we're going to the playoffs," he said with a happy laugh.

Wishbone barked. "You bet we are, Joe! Have I told you yet how satisfying it is to see all our years of hard work together finally pay off?"

The Sequoyah players reached the edge of the field. Excited fans surrounded them. Wishbone stayed close to Joe. He was thinking about his friend getting hit on the head.

I'm sure I've come across something like this before. What was it? Wishbone raised a hind leg and scratched behind one ear. Then he scratched his head. *Aha! I've got it! I'm thinking of Hank Morgan.*

Hank Morgan is the hero of a terrific novel called *A Connecticut Yankee in King Arthur's Court.* Hank gets clobbered on the head during a fight. He's knocked out cold. He wakes up to discover that he's traveled back in time over thirteen hundred years! He's gone all the way back to the sixth century!

The well-loved, nineteenth-century American

writer Mark Twain wrote *A Connecticut Yankee in King Arthur's Court.* It was published in 1889. Twain wrote this novel in the first person—as if Hank Morgan were telling the story himself. The novel begins in the city of Hartford, Connecticut, in the late 1800s.

Chapter Two

Wishbone pictured Hartford, Connecticut, in the year 1885. Horse-drawn carriages clattered up and down the busy cobblestone streets. Men wearing business suits and round bowler hats rushed in and out of the many banks. They regularly looked at the gold watches that they wore tucked into their vest pockets. Young women hurried to their jobs at the telephone and insurance companies. Their long, pleated skirts brushed over the paving stones.

Every morning, dozens of boys sold newspapers on the downtown street corners. "Get the early-bird news!" they shouted. "Read all about it!" As dusk fell over the city every evening, the new electric streetlights would suddenly blaze. The older residents of Hartford would stare at the lights and say, "Well, how 'bout that! They've turned night into day!"

Wishbone put himself into the middle of this nine-teenth-century scene of hustle and bustle. It was the Machine Age—a time of inventions and progress. It was a time when someone with a clever mind and a lot of ambition could get ahead. Wishbone imagined himself as just that type of person. He was a man in his early thirties. He was Hank Morgan of Hartford, Connecticut, and he was about to tell his story. . . .

I am an American—a purebred Connecticut Yankee from the tip of my nose to the end of my tail. A Yankee is someone who was born or raised in the north of the United States. I was born in the countryside near the city of Hartford. My father worked as a blacksmith; my uncle worked as a horse doctor. I did both jobs as a young pup until my four paws itched for something better. I wanted to make my mark on the world. More than anything else, I wanted to be a master mechanic—an expert who designed new machines and built them from scratch.

One day, I trotted over to the great firearms factory in Hartford. There, workers made all kinds of mechanical objects. I found the man who ran the place and tapped him on the leg.

"I want to learn the mechanic's trade," I said. "I know I'll do a good job of it." With my muzzle set firm and my tail wagging, I gave just the right impression. I was determined and eager. In fact, I'd have looked irresistible to anyone who knew his business. I got myself a job.

You can bet your bottom dollar that I learned the mechanic's trade in that factory. I learned to make tools and gadgets of every kind. I learned to put together all types of motors. Before long, I could build an engine, a locomotive, or design a telegraph system with one paw tied behind my back. When someone needed a labor-saving machine that didn't yet exist, who got called? Hank Morgan—you can bet your bottom dollar on that, too. I could invent and build whatever anyone needed. It was all as easy for me as rolling off a log or scratching a flea bite behind my ear.

As soon as I learned the ropes in the factory, I started climbing. I wanted to be top dog in that place. Soon I became the head superintendent of the whole kit and caboodle. More than two thousand workers called me "boss."

Life looked good to me—like a warm biscuit sitting in my dish. I had my job, my buddies on the factory baseball team, and a sweetheart who worked at the telephone company. I'd phone her there every week. I'd say, "Hello, operator!," just to hear her lovely voice come back to me with a "Hello, Hank!"

I had all kinds of responsibilities at the factory. For example, a fellow in my position—even one who disliked violence as much as I did—had to take on troublemakers. It was my job to see to the safety of all my factory workers. When a bully threatened to slow down work or harm a crew member, I'd ask him to step outside and settle the score. I never lost more than a whisker or a tuft of fur in those fights—until one morning when I had to take on a mechanic we called Hercules.

Hercules had the temper of an alley cat. He enjoyed picking on the youngest and newest workers. I told him to meet me on a patch of grass in back of the factory. When we stood facing each other, he towered over me like a giant. He had arms as thick as my belly. That mean bully didn't give me a chance to take off my leather work apron, remove my protective goggles, or loosen my plaid tie. Hercules just grabbed a steel crowbar and swung it at

15

my head as if it were a baseball bat. He meant to hit a home run.

Whack!

I heard the bones in my head crack. Every piece of my skull smacked into its neighbor. The world went dark. I didn't know or feel anything else.

I finally woke up, not aware of exactly how much time had passed. I lay flat on the grass. The afternoon sun was still shining. I immediately tried to move my four legs and head. I wanted to find out if my personal machinery—my body—still worked. I seemed to be in one piece.

I saw my work goggles lying nearby. Nothing else around me looked familiar. A large oak tree towered above me. In front of me stretched a wide, country landscape. There were flowering meadows; green, rolling hills; and patches of woods. To my surprise, I didn't see the factory or Hercules or any of the other men. I sniffed the air, hoping that would help me to figure out where I was. I picked up a few scents—clover, damp soil, birds, and . . . very close by . . . a horse!

I turned my head so quickly to look over my shoulder that my ears flapped. My eyes popped open to twice their normal size.

Right behind me stood a horse. On the horse sat a man who seemed to have popped out of a picture book. He wore a suit of old-time iron armor. It covered him from head to toe. His helmet looked like an upside-down bucket with slits for his eyes to see through. He carried a shield, sword, and a giant-sized spear. His horse, too, wore a costume. A white mask covered half the animal's head. Red and white silk cloth hung all around its body, like a fancy bedspread.

16

I stood up and wagged my tail with approval. "Nifty costume," I said. "I reckon you belong with the circus."

The fellow answered with a question. "Fair sir, will ye joust?"

"Will I *what?*" I asked him.

"Will ye try a battle of weapons for land or lady or for—"

The fur on my back bristled. I wasn't in the mood for fun and games. My head still ached badly. All I wanted to do was to figure out how far from Hartford I'd ended up, and who had moved me to where I was. I barked. "What poppycock are you giving me? Get on back to your circus—or I'll report you to the Hartford police."

What did Mr. Iron-Suit do? He moved back a few hundred yards. Then, he turned and came rushing at me as hard and fast as he could. He bent his bucket helmet down nearly to his horse's neck. His long, sharp spear pointed straight ahead. I knew he meant business. I pushed off with my hind legs, and sprang up as high as I could. I was up the oak tree when he arrived.

"Ye are the captive of my spear!" the fellow shouted.

I couldn't disagree with him on that point.

He jabbed his weapon into the oak branches so hard that he ripped off a dozen twigs and nearly shaved my tail. He yelled all the while. "Ye are my property. Give up and come with me or I shall slay you and cut you into a thousand pieces!"

Anyone with a five-cent brain could see that he had the advantage over me. I judged it best to humor him along—to do what he asked.

"I'll come with you," I called down, "if you give me your word not to harm me."

"I promise on the honor of my sword," he answered.

I figured I wasn't going to get a better deal, so I jumped down from the tree. Keeping one eye on that spear, I picked up my goggles with my teeth. I brushed off my shirt and tie. A few moments later, I was trotting at a comfortable pace alongside Mr. Bucket-Helmet and his costumed horse.

We marched over fields, crossed brooks, and went up hills. I didn't recognize any of the places we passed. This puzzled me. We never came to a circus, or even saw a sign of one. After a while, I gave up the circus idea. I figured that my escort had escaped from an asylum—one of those special hospitals where they cared for insane— mentally ill—people. Yet we never came to an asylum, either.

I was one hundred percent puzzled. My head hurt from doing so much guesswork. As a trained mechanic, I needed exact information. It made my hide itch like the dickens not to know just what my situation was.

"How far are we from Hartford?" I asked.

Mr. Iron-Sides kept riding, with his bucket-face looking straight ahead. "I know of no such place," he said.

Either he's lying, I thought, *or he's got more than a few loose screws in his helmet.* I glanced at his spear and decided to keep quiet.

At the end of an hour, I breathed a sigh of relief to see a town stretched out in the next valley, near a winding river. On a hill overlooking the town stood a huge, gray-stone fortress. A dozen towers rose up from around its thick walls.

I pointed to the town and fortress. "Bridgeport, Connecticut?" I asked. "Or New Haven, maybe?"

My escort shook his bucket head. "Nay. Camelot."

Camelot? I shrugged my furred shoulders. I knew I'd never heard of a town in Connecticut by that name. *It must be the name of the asylum,* I thought.

We continued to trot through the soft, peaceful-looking landscape. When we got close to the town, the first signs of life appeared. We passed tiny, gloomy-looking huts with roofs made of a thick layer of straw called thatch. I saw people, too. The men had uncombed, long hair that fell over their faces. Both men and women wore sandals and plain-looking rough linen robes that hung down below their knees. The small children ran around naked—although no one seemed to notice but me.

These people gave me something new to wonder about. They stared at me; they pointed at my clothes; they ran into their huts and brought out their relatives for a look. Yet nobody gave a hoot about Mr. Iron-Suit's

costume. They bowed politely to him without getting so much as a nod in return. I couldn't make heads or tails of their strange behavior.

I followed my escort along the town's crooked, unpaved alleyways. The mud there was more than paw-deep. Children and hogs played together in the muck. The whole place smelled of rotting garbage and unwashed bodies.

Suddenly my ears pricked up. I heard a very distant sound of military music. It came nearer . . . nearer . . . still nearer. When we reached the edge of the town, a grand parade came into full view.

I barked with delight at what I saw: dozens of horses covered with their silk bedspreads; all the riders wearing full suits of armor; colored banners; helmets with large feathers called plumes; and highly polished bugles sparkling in the last rays of the sun.

"Just look at that!" I exclaimed to my escort. "It's all your friends from the asylum in a picture-book parade!"

Mr. Helmet-Head didn't even look in my direction. Yet his bad manners didn't get under my fur. I figured our little adventure together would soon end. He would get back together with the other patients. I would then tell the asylum's director that the patient was back. Afterward, I would hire a coach to drive me back to Hartford in time for a "Hello, operator!" call to my sweetheart.

We followed the parade up the hill until we arrived at the breezy height of the gray-stone fortress. Costumed guards stood in front of the fortress with their long-handled battle-axes. There was a loud blowing of bugles. Several guards swung open the gigantic iron gates. Others lowered a heavy drawbridge over the deep, water-filled moat that surrounded the stone walls of the fortress.

The parade went over the bridge and then under the high arches of the gateway. I trotted along in time to the bugle music. My tail swayed back and forth like one of the silk banners. The day had begun badly—with a humdinger of a whack on the head. Yet it was ending quite nicely—or so I thought.

Once past the gateway, I found myself in a large cobblestone courtyard. The building's walls and the towers of different sizes stretched up into the sky on all sides. The riders began to get down from their horses with the help of servants. Perfumed ladies in satin gowns came out of the building to greet them. The place was hopping with action, the clanking of armor, cheerful displays of color, and a completely pleasant sense of confusion. After the knights took off their armor, they escorted the ladies inside.

My four paws carried me quickly to one side of the courtyard. I kept an eye out for a normal person who could direct me to the asylum authorities. I noticed a slim boy in shrimp-colored tights that made him look like a split carrot. The rest of his gear was all blue silk and ruffles. A pink-satin cap topped his blond curls. He looked fancy enough to be a picture. What I liked most about him was his intelligent, curious, even bold gaze. With one look, he saw all of me—from my welder's goggles, which I had pushed high onto my forehead, to my mud-caked paws. He smiled in a careless but friendly way, and he stepped toward me.

"I'd like to ask your help," I said in a low voice as soon as he came close enough. "I need to see the asylum's head keeper."

"Marry! Fair sir, me seemeth—"

I tried to nod politely while I interrupted him. "Excuse my rudeneess, young fellow, but . . . are you also a patient in this asylum? Or are you just here on a visit?"

"I am a page," he told me.

My tail twitched with irritation. *Another patient. This one thinks he's a page—one of those boys who does errands for a king or queen.*

While I glanced around, looking for a more reliable source of information, the boy began to chat. He clearly wanted to be friends. He told me all about himself. He asked a dozen questions about me and my clothes— although he wasn't the type to wait for answers. He just chatted on and on. I listened to him with half an ear— until one sentence caught my attention.

"I was born in the winter of the year 513," he said.

Cold chills crept over my hide. My whiskers stood on end. When I spoke, my voice sounded weak. "Maybe I didn't hear you quite right. Say it again—and say it sloowwwly. In what year were you born?"

The boy smiled pleasantly. "513."

My fur bristled. "513! That would make you one thousand, three hundred and seventy-two years old!" I snorted. "You don't look it!"

The page shook his head as if he were sorry about my poor mathematical skills. "Forsooth, sir, I am but fifteen years old."

My mouth went dry. I tried to catch my breath. I spoke hoarsely. "Come on, my boy. I'm a stranger here, and I need an honest friend. Be truthful with me. Are you in your right mind?"

The boy nodded in a sincere manner.

I pointed to the crowd in the courtyard. "Are all these other people in their right minds?"

He nodded again.

My heart began to pound so hard that I could see the fur on my chest bobbing up and down. I asked, "This isn't an asylum where insane people are cared for?"

The boy shook his head. "Nay."

I swallowed hard and asked yet another question. "Tell me—according to your best calculation, what is the date today?"

The page squatted down, looked me straight in the eye, and said, "June 20, 528."

I waited a minute to let that idea sink into my brain. "Well, then," I whispered, "either I am insane, or something just as awful has happened." I stared hard at the boy. "Now, tell me, honest and true—exactly where am I?"

For an instant, a look of surprise flickered across the boy's face. He couldn't understand why I needed to ask such a question. Then he leaned even closer to my muzzle—as if to confirm that he spoke the truth. He replied slowly, and with complete certainty, "You are in England—in the royal court of King Arthur."

Wishbone's Dictionary for Anyone in the Dark About the Dark Ages

alas!	expression of sorrow or pity
Camelot	according to legend, it was the location of King Arthur's royal court and castle-fortress
chain mail	flexible, protective material, made of tiny metal links, usually worn under suits of armor
Dark Ages	period of time in European history after the downfall of the once-great Roman Empire. The Dark Ages (A.D. 476 to 1000), which included King Arthur's time, was also a period when learning and culture were in a decline in Europe. There are no complete written records of how people lived then, or what their everyday use of language was like. Therefore, many writers, including Mark Twain, used the clothing, customs, and language of the Middle Ages (from about A.D. 500 to 1500) to represent the Dark Ages.
democracy	government that is run by the people who live under it
doth	does
dungeon	dark underground prison

25

—eth	a verb ending used in many older English texts, including those of Shakespeare. Writers often use this verb ending to create entertaining dialogue that sounds old. An example: *Wishbone waketh, feeleth hunger, and barketh most loudly.*
forsooth!	indeed!
freeman	anyone who was not a noble, Church official, or slave. Freemen included peasant farmers and craftsmen such as carpenters and blacksmiths.
hath	has
henceforth	from now on
jest	prank, or humorous remark
joust	contest with weapons between two knights on horseback
King Arthur	according to folklore and legend, a famous king who lived in the land that is now modern-day England. His story is based on tales about a sixth-century military leader.
knight	soldier on horseback who belonged to the noble class of society and served another noble of higher rank
knighthood	all knights as a group, or category, in society
list	long, dirt playing field on which jousts took place
marry!	expression of surprise or amusement
me thinks	I think

moat	deep, wide trench, usually filled with water, that enclosed the outside walls of a castle and served as protection against invaders
monarchy	a government that is ruled by members of a royal family
nay	no
noble	a person of high rank or title who is a member of one of the ruling families in a society
page	boy who worked for a knight or who was training to become a knight
perchance	perhaps
quest	journey of adventure
sire	title used to address a man of authority
subject	person under the authority or control of someone else
sundial	instrument showing the time of day by means of a shadow cast by a non-moving marker onto a flat surface or cylinder in the sun
'tis	it is
tournament	series of contests, attended by spectators, during which knights tested their strength, courage, and skill with weapons
wherefore	therefore
ye	you
ye wit	you know
yonder	indicating something distant but still within view

Chapter Three

In the royal court of King Arthur? In the royal court of King Arthur!

The words rang inside my head. My four legs wobbled. I felt my heart sink.

"I shall never see my sweetheart or my friends again," I whispered. "Never, never again! They will not be born for more than thirteen hundred years."

I slumped down to my haunches. I covered my eyes with my front paws. I don't know why, but something deep inside me believed the boy. My emotions—you might say—believed him. Yet my practical mind didn't. My mind soon began to put up a terrible fuss.

Go on! my mind told me. *Try to prove this is King Arthur's court and not Hartford, Connecticut. Get some hard facts. You can't rely on what anyone here says. This is the craziest place this side of the Mississippi River.*

The boy, who was still squatting next to me, took hold of one of my paws. "Are ye ill? Ye tremble like a dry leaf."

I could have skipped the comparison, but I appreciated

the kindness in his eyes. I took a deep breath. I gave myself a shake hard enough to make my ears flap. It helped to focus my thoughts.

"Don't worry your curly-haired head about me," I said to the boy. "I just need a few minutes of deep thinking."

I stood up and trotted to a nearby wall. I started to pace up and down its length. My nails clicked sharply on the cobblestones. By luck, I came up with a really clever idea.

I had once read that a total eclipse of the sun had taken place on June 21 in the year 528. It began at exactly three minutes past noon. I also knew that no solar eclipse was due to occur in the year 1885. The boy claimed that the current date was June 20, 528. Therefore, if an eclipse took place at three minutes past noon the following day, the lad was indeed speaking the truth.

"I'll have my proof tomorrow," I said, "as long as curiosity and worry don't kill me before then."

I turned my thoughts next to my current situation. I needed to be alert and ready to make the most of it. I sat down and studied the courtyard scene in front of me. People were moving out of the courtyard and into the castle. My tail slowly thumped—as it always did when I thought hard. A moment later, I had made up my mind about two important things.

First, I said to myself, *what if it turns out to be 1885 and I'm in an asylum for insane folks and can't get away? In that case, I'll just make myself boss of the asylum. If I don't succeed within three weeks, my name isn't Hank Morgan. Second, what if it really is 528? In that case, I will become boss of the whole country within three months. After all, I'll have a headstart in education over everyone else by more than thirteen hundred years!*

I wasn't the type to waste time when my mind was made up and when I had work to do. I got up and trotted quickly back to the boy.

"Now, Clarence—" I said.

He looked confused.

I felt impatient. "I know that's probably not your name, but we're pressed for time. So if it's all right with you, let's just go with Clarence."

Being spunky and curious, Clarence nodded eagerly.

I continued. "I need you to fill me in on some details. Who brought me here? And what will happen next?"

Clarence took a deep breath. Then he began to talk faster than a horse running around a racetrack. That boy's tongue could move faster than my tail. I finally got the information I needed.

According to Clarence, I was the prisoner of Sir Kay, a great nobleman and knight. Like all knights, Sir Kay loved to go off to distant lands to fight wars of any kind. When there was no war to fight in, he and the other knights roamed the countryside looking for dragons, giants, and new knights to fight. They brought their prisoners—he paused and pointed at those around us—back to the castle-fortress. Later, they held a show-and-tell in front of the king's court. At the moment, the members of the court were in the castle's great hall—the large meeting room of the royal court—finishing dinner. Afterward, they would drink more, talk, and exhibit the prisoners—including yours truly—to the king and queen.

I was about to ask Clarence what happened after show-and-tell. Just then, a castle guard interrupted us. He announced that all prisoners must go immediately into the great hall.

"Come with me," Clarence said. "I'll show you what to do."

My four paws followed Clarence's two silk slippers through an arched doorway and along an empty stone passageway. The other prisoners, about twenty, stumbled along with us. Their physical condition made my whiskers tremble. Poor fellows! They had been hacked at and carved up by swords in a frightful way. They were suffering sharp pain, hunger, and thirst. Yet not one of them let out a moan or a groan.

I was forced to conclude that these other prisoners were all rascals. They must have treated other people the same way in the past. So they did not expect any better treatment than what they were getting now.

Clarence turned to me. "Be most careful of what you do now," he whispered. "This is the great hall."

What strange sights I saw before me! The room was huge and almost bare. Its walls rose up so high that the banners hanging from the arched ceiling beams floated in a sort of twilight. At one end of the hall, musicians sat on a balcony behind a stone railing. At the opposite end of the hall, a second balcony held women clothed in dazzling gowns. The main decoration in the huge room was some large woven rugs called tapestries—they hung on the walls. They all showed battle scenes. I wouldn't have paid a dollar for the whole bunch of them, but I guessed the king thought they were great works of art.

The strong odors of roasted meat and wine filled the air. My empty stomach grumbled.

Clarence made his way to a carved wood stool. "Stand on this," he whispered to me. He stood close by.

Pushing off with my hind legs, I jumped up onto the stool. From there I had a fine view.

31

In the middle of the hall was an oak table the size of a circus ring. According to Clarence, this was the famous Round Table where King Arthur and his knights gathered to talk and to plan their war strategy. The knights had exchanged their armor for clothes of colors bright enough to make me blink. They all wore fancy hats at the table, except when they spoke directly to the king. Then each speaker would lift his hat just a little as he began to talk. It was a sign of respect to the king. Along the walls, guards in armor stood as still as statues.

I quickly discovered that Round Table talk consisted of stories about battles won and prisoners captured. As far as I could tell, the knights didn't have duels to settle arguments. No, they fought just to fight. They reminded me of children who met by chance, and, in the same instant, said, "Bet I can beat you!" Yet the knights were not children. They were big knuckleheads who took great pride in having deadly adventures.

"Nine of the greatest giants in Spain surrounded me," a small, red-haired knight claimed. "With just two strokes of my sword, I cut off all their heads. Then I took a long, deep breath and blew them piece by piece across the sea to Africa!"

All in all, I doubted there were enough brains in the great hall to bait a fishhook with. Of course, the knights didn't need brains in a place like that. On the contrary— brains would have gotten in the way.

Yet I still found something attractive and lovable about these people. They listened to one another's stories so seriously—no matter how whopping the exaggerations and lies were. I also saw signs of fine courage in every knight's face. In some, I also saw true honor and kindness. That made me silence my criticism of them.

I tapped Clarence on the arm. "Is that one King Arthur?" With my muzzle, I pointed to the tallest, most handsome man at the table.

He was about my age, and he sat on the grandest chair. He had truly royal posture—straight, but graceful. His clothes were made from expensive fabrics. He wore both his chestnut-brown hair and his beard long. He had a large, straight nose. The man certainly looked like a king. However, I doubted that he had even a teaspoonful more sense than his subjects.

Clarence nodded. "So it is—he is our lord, master, and king."

I couldn't help snorting softly. "Just hold your breath, my boy. We Yankees will put an end to all the masters and kings. Of course, you'll have to hold your breath for over twelve hundred years to see that happen." I wagged my tail with glee at the thought.

Clarence didn't have a clue about what I meant. Still, he smiled as pleasantly as always. I asked him to tell me about the key players on King Arthur's team.

Clarence pointed to a large, handsome man with dark curly hair. "That is Sir Launcelot," Clarence whispered. "He's the bravest and most skillful knight of the entire Round Table."

Next, Clarence pointed to a thin old man with a long, stringy, white beard and sharp eyes. He wore a red-velvet robe and a black-and-gold hat that looked like an upside-down ice-cream cone.

"That's Merlin," Clarence said. "He is the mighty court magician."

Well, wouldn't ya know! I thought. *These people believe in giants and dragons. So it's only natural that they should keep a magician on the royal payroll.* My tail stopped wagging. I didn't like the sneaky look in Merlin's beady eyes.

Last, Clarence pointed out a lady in the balcony. Her big jewels and showy coral-silk gown clearly proved to everyone in the place that she was a big deal. She had almond-shaped green eyes. Some of her long blond hair fell down around her shoulders. The rest was piled on top of her head and fastened with silver clips.

"She is Queen Guenever," Clarence explained. With a sad sigh, he added, "She will decide whether you live or die."

My fur stood on end. My nose twitched. I stared at Clarence. "Die! Who put that choice on tonight's menu? I don't— Ouch!"

Clarence had jabbed a finger into my hide to silence me. "Your turn has come!" he whispered. "Sir Kay speaks next. Here is what you must do. . . ."

With his head pressed against my muzzle, Clarence quickly whispered instructions. He told me exactly how to move, and exactly what to say.

Sir Kay rose from his chair and lifted his hat in respect to the king. I was relieved to see that he looked no less normal than anyone else without his armor. I hopped down from my stool. The other prisoners stepped back so that everyone could see me.

The knights and ladies gasped. A few screamed and ran out of the hall. Shocked comments started flying around the room.

"Forsooth! What most strange and terrible clothes he weareth!"

"Never has the world seen such frightful armor!"

"Frightful?" I said. "Forsooth not! I mean, indeed not! This is a top-of-the-line welding apron and goggles. They cost me seven dollars!"

"Shh!" Clarence nudged me with his toe.

I decided to ignore the insults. As Clarence had told me, I dropped to my haunches, stretched out my front legs, and bowed my head deeply. I stayed in that embarrassing position while Sir Kay fired up his story-engine with me as fuel.

"In an unknown land of giants and dragons," Sir Kay began, "I challenged this very monster for the glory of our queen. I quickly realized that he wore magical clothes. No sword or dagger or crossbow could make even a scratch in such an ugly and powerful costume."

The great hall echoed with the sounds of amazement. I took one peek at the crowd and saw that every mouth was opened wide enough to catch flies.

Sir Kay continued. "I was determined to defeat this monster. I prayed for strength, and my prayer broke the magical spell. After a three-hour battle, I killed all thirteen knights who were with this monster."

I nearly choked listening to all this phoney baloney. I kept quiet, though, because Clarence had advised me not to disagree with anything the knight said.

Sir Kay's tall tale went on.

"This monster, with its deadly sharp tusks and claws, sprang to the top of a tree. The tree stood no less than two hundred feet high. I lifted a rock as large as a cow and threw it at the monster. My aim was perfect. I hit the monster hard. It fell to the ground—every bone in its dreadful body broken!"

Sir Kay paused for dramatic effect. The listeners nodded, clucked their tongues, and "ooohed" and "ahed" with admiration. They believed every word. Sir Kay finished his story with style.

"I could have slain this horrible monster with a

single slash of my swift sword. Yet it is such a weird-looking beast that I spared its life. I carried it back to Camelot to show it to the royal court."

Sir Kay's show ended with a low bow to Queen Guenever. She nodded gracefully in response. According to Clarence, that was the signal for my own performance to begin.

No one loved a theatrical show more than Hank Morgan. So I threw everything I had into my short solo act. I lifted my chest off the floor. I raised my front paws toward the queen. I pleaded. "Oh, Your Majesty, Mistress, and Queen—I deliver myself into your hands. I throw myself at your most royal feet. Sir Kay has defeated me on the field of battle by his strength and skill. I breathlessly await your royal word to decide my future."

The queen leaned forward in the balcony. Her long silk scarves floated around her shoulders. She opened her mouth to speak. . . .

"Wait!"

I and everyone else in the huge hall turned toward the sound of the high-pitched, harsh-sounding voice. Merlin, the magician, stood up. He pulled on his scraggly beard and pointed a bony finger at me. His mean eyes sent a shiver all along my spine and tail.

"Beware!" Merlin screeched. "One who wears such strange and ugly armor is under the spell of an evil magician. You must put this prisoner to death!"

That old buzzard! I thought. *He's just afraid of competition from another magician.* No one would take him seriously, I decided.

To my horror, the queen nodded her agreement with Merlin. Then, adding insult to injury, she yawned, as if the entertainment had become dull. The musicians immediately started to play a jolly tune. The knights raised their wineglasses and drank.

Everyone seemed to forget about me—except the armed guards. Two of them grabbed my front paws and dragged me from the hall. I twisted and snarled like a grizzly bear caught in a trap. It was no use. They hauled me along a passageway. They pulled me down a long, dark, narrow flight of steps. I was bounced and scraped against the rough stones.

Above me, I heard light, rapid footsteps.

"Alas! I am filled with sorrow!" Clarence called out. "I gave you all the best advice I did have." His voice echoed in the stairwell. "Lose not heart! Have courage! I will visit you tomorrow. I will bring news."

Lose not heart! I was close to losing my *head!* My mind was in a terrible state of panic and misery. My body felt just as bad after being dragged down all those stairs. Under my furred hide, every muscle and joint throbbed with pain.

We arrived finally in the dungeon. It was a dark, damp, cramped place filled with the foul odors of dirt and disease. The guards shoved me into a tiny cell and then slammed the heavy iron door shut. After a few minutes, my eyes began to adjust to the darkness. I could make out what else occupied the cell besides me. I had some moldy straw for a bed, and a family of rats to keep me company.

Despair filled my heart. Fear gripped my brain. Yet I was so tired that not even these strong emotions could keep me awake. I fell into a deep sleep.

I heard nothing, saw nothing, and smelled nothing until the sounds of chains clanking and metal scraping began to awaken me. I felt someone or something shake me. I opened one eye. I saw a face—a boy's face. It was Clarence.

I groaned. "You again! I was hoping this whole Camelot business was just a bad dream." I sighed and began to scratch the crop of flea bites I had collected during the night. "What time is it?" I asked.

"Ah, 'tis late in your life," Clarence said. He shook his head sadly. "It is nine in the morning."

The gloomy expression on Clarence's face frightened me. My heart began to race.

"What do you mean by ''tis late in your life'?" I asked.

A tear fell from each of Clarence's eyes as he spoke. "At noon today, you are to be burned at the stake!"

Now poor Hank Morgan has just two things on his mind—a horrible punishment, followed by death.

Meanwhile, back in Oakdale, I'm still thinking about the great soccer game.

Chapter Four

Wishbone joined Joe and several dozen other students who stood on the sidewalk in front of the Sequoyah Middle School. It was Friday afternoon. The school week had just ended.

"Hey, Joe!" someone called out. "That was a great game yesterday! Congratulations!"

Wishbone saw his friend Samantha Kepler nod in agreement. "It sure was a great game!" she said. Sam's blond ponytail bobbed up and down as she nodded her head. Her hazel eyes sparkled. "The way you intercepted that pass was amazing, Joe. And that goal in the last second of the game—perfect!"

Sam was one of Joe's two best friends. They were in some of the same classes in the sixth grade. Sam was smart, fun to be with, and kind to everyone. Wishbone had a special liking for her. Sam could almost always sense when a dog needed a snack or a good rub behind the ears.

Wishbone's tail waved back and forth like a banner. "I really love all this victory chitchat. Shall I share some thoughts about Joe's one-on-one practice sessions with you-know-who? I—"

"Look—it's Ryan Clark and Anna Valdez," Joe said.

He pointed to a thin, red-haired boy, and a slim, athletic-looking girl with dark curly hair. They had just stepped out of the school building. Each carried a stack of papers. They began to pass out the sheets to the kids standing nearby.

"*Sports Report!* Read all about it!" Anna called out. "Get your *Sports Report* right here!"

"I think Anna and Ryan are two of the neatest kids in the eighth grade," Sam whispered to Joe. "They're both really good writers. They decided the school needed a newsletter just for sports. So they began to publish one this year. They do it all by themselves on one of the school's computers."

Joe agreed. "I can't wait to see what they wrote about yesterday's game."

Wishbone's ears pricked up. "I bet it's a front-page story, Joe. Huge headline, big photo—the whole nine yards. Oops! Wrong sport."

"I'll get us some copies," Sam said.

She walked over to Anna and got two copies of the newsletter. She started to read one as she walked back toward Joe. Wishbone watched her face. He saw her expression change—from eager to puzzled to disappointed.

What? Wishbone wondered. *No photo?*

Sam sighed as she handed Joe a copy of the single-sheet newsletter. "Look on the back," she said, "at the bottom."

Joe quickly glanced at the sheet. "Is this it?" he asked. He read aloud from the very bottom of the page.

"'Thursday's soccer game: Sequoyah, two. Franklin, one.'"

Wishbone stopped wagging his tail. He sat down on the pavement. "Folks, you are looking at one very disappointed dog."

"I don't understand why Anna and Ryan didn't write a whole story about the game," Sam said. "It was so exciting." She saw the unhappy look on Joe's face. "Well, there's no way in the world they can skip writing about next Thursday's playoff."

Sam looked at her watch. "I've got to go. I'm meeting my dad—five minutes ago." She waved as she started to jog down the sidewalk. "See you later."

Joe was still looking at the newsletter when Ryan Clark walked up to him.

"You're Joe Talbot, aren't you?" Ryan asked.

Joe nodded. He had never talked to Ryan before.

"Sorry we couldn't get a full story about the soccer game into the newsletter," Ryan said. "We can't cover any games on Thursday afternoons. That's when we put the whole newsletter together so we can hand it out on Friday." He shrugged. "Well, that's the way it goes with a two-person business like ours."

Joe nodded again. Then something occurred to

him. "But the sixth-grade playoffs begin next Thursday afternoon. You mean you're not going to cover our big soccer game?"

Wishbone barked twice and groaned loudly. *I hope Ryan realizes that was my version of an angry letter to the editor.*

Ryan thought for a moment. He shook his head. "Sorry—we can't do it. Tuesday is boys' basketball and the playoff for field hockey. Wednesday is an important football game. We can't mess around with the newsletter production schedule next week. There's just too much stuff going on."

Joe tried to hide his disappointment in front of the older kids. "Right. Well . . ."

Ryan turned to hand a newsletter to one of his friends. Over his shoulder he said to Joe, "Anyway, I heard you played great yesterday."

The crowd on the sidewalk broke up. Joe and Wishbone headed toward home. A block from school, they caught up with David Barnes, Joe's other best friend. He had short, dark, curly hair. David was a computer expert and the top science student in their class at school. He lived next door to Joe and Wishbone.

Joe handed David the newsletter. "Ryan and Anna couldn't get a story about yesterday's game into *Sports Report*," he said. "What's worse, they won't have time to write anything about next Thursday's playoff game, except maybe give the final score." Joe kicked a small stone with the toe of his sneaker. The stone sailed down the sidewalk. "I can't believe it. This is the best season that a Sequoyah sixth-grade soccer team has ever had!"

David examined the newsletter carefully as they walked. The style of type was simple, and it was the same on both sides of the sheet. There were no photos or special design elements. The margins were narrow. The newsletter had an overall dull look. It was hard to tell where some articles ended and others began.

Wishbone noticed the look of concentration on David's face.

"You know, technically, *Sports Report* is like something out of the Dark Ages," David said.

Wishbone paused to sniff a tree, but he didn't miss a word of the conversation.

Dark Ages? Oh, yeah, the period after the fall of the Roman Empire. The Dark Ages lasted approximately from the year 476 to the year 1000. That includes the time of King Arthur.

David continued. "With a decent computer and a good desktop-publishing program, you could do a much better job. You could design great visuals and use photos. You could have headlines in different sizes and use different type styles. You could arrange columns and margins that look really slick, like they do in a major sports magazine."

Joe looked doubtful. "Sure, all that would be great. But Anna and Ryan don't have time to report on the playoff game next Thursday. Who's going to write about the game after it's over?"

David looked surprised. "That's no problem. You and I could do it—easily."

"You mean write something for the *Sports Report?*" Joe asked.

David shook his head. "No! I'm talking about putting together our *own* newsletter for the soccer playoffs. I'd take notes during the game. Then we'd write up the story that evening." David's eyes sparkled.

"Maybe there would be time for a quick interview with the winning coach. And you might want to write something about the whole season—a sort of soccer overview."

A shivering sensation ran up and down Wishbone's furred back. "An idea is starting to catch fire here. I can feel the heat. My own thrills-and-chills engine is already revving up."

Joe stopped walking. "David, could we do all that on your computer?"

David turned toward Joe. "Sure. It would be easy— and fun. Of course, we'd have to get the design and layout all ready beforehand. We'd think up a neat name and then create a really special logo." He grinned at Joe. "You know, we have a whole weekend to try to come up with something great."

The boys walked along for a few minutes without speaking. They were both thinking about their own ideas for the project.

Wishbone looked from Joe to David, then back at Joe. "It's a brilliant idea. Go for it, guys!"

Joe nodded as if he were having a conversation with himself. Then he held out his hand to David. "Partner— let's do it!"

A first-rate report on the soccer playoffs, one that uses the latest in computer graphics—that is a brilliant idea.

Meanwhile, someone else desperately needs a brilliant idea—Hank Morgan. In his prison cell, he's just heard that he's been sentenced to death.

Chapter Five

"**B**urned at the stake!"

A shock went through my entire body when I repeated Clarence's words. I started to collapse in a heap of misery on my bed of straw. Fortunately, the thought of being attacked again by the prison flea population kept me standing on my four feet. I didn't give up hope completely.

"Ah, Clarence!" I said. "You're the only friend I've got here." I looked at him closely. "You *are* my friend, aren't you?"

Clarence nodded long and hard.

"Don't fail me, my boy," I went on. "Help me find some way of escaping from this terrible place."

"Escape!" Clarence exclaimed. "Do but listen to thyself! The hallways and doors are guarded by armed men!"

"How many guards?" I asked. "Not many—I hope."

Clarence's eyes filled with terror. He turned as white as a clean handkerchief. He shook like a dry leaf.

"Escape is impossible," he whispered, "for . . . for another reason. But it's a secret."

"What's the matter?" I asked. "You look as if you're going all to pieces—and you're not the one who's about to be burned alive."

Clarence sat down on the filthy cell floor. "I dare not tell you! I dare not!"

I patted his knee. "Come on, Clarence—be brave. Speak out!"

Clarence hesitated. He crept to the door of the cell and listened. Then he tiptoed back to me. With his mouth to my ear, he whispered, "Merlin has cast a magical spell on this dungeon!"

I couldn't control myself. I lay down and rolled over onto my back. With my paws shaking in the air, I had a good laugh, my most enjoyable one in—literally—ages.

"Cast a spell?!" I shouted. "Merlin? That cheap old humbug! That bumbling phoney!"

Poor Clarence just about fainted right on top of me. He gasped. He got on his knees in front of me and began to beg.

"Oh, beware! Those are such awful words! These stone walls will tumble down upon us if you say such bad things. Take them back before it is too late! I beg you!"

This strange behavior got me thinking. I sat up. My tail started to thump in that nice, slow, thinking rhythm.

Suppose everybody around here is just as afraid of Merlin's pretend magic, I thought. *Then certainly a modern, educated fellow like myself can take advantage of such a situation.*

When I stood on my four paws a few minutes later, I had come up with a plan—or at least a good start on one. I put my face so close to Clarence's that my whiskers brushed his cheeks.

"Do you know why I laughed?" I asked.

"No," Clarence answered. "But in the name of all that is good, do it no more!"

"I laughed," I said, "because *I'm* a magician myself!"

I studied Clarence's reaction. He caught his breath. He scooted back against the wall of the cell. His face took on a very, very respectful look.

Clarence's reaction told me what I needed to know. People in the castle would believe whatever phoney nonsense they were told. *Hank,* I thought, *get ready to dish out the nonsense.*

"Listen, Clarence," I said, beginning my ridiculous story, "I've known Merlin for years—seven hundred years, to be exact. Every century or so, he pops up wherever I am—India, Egypt, England. He's always taking on a new name—Moe, Mike, Merlin. He's always getting in my way, always screeching like an alley cat. To tell you the truth, I'm really tired of him."

I paused again to test Clarence's reaction. He stared at me with eyes as big as golf balls.

I went on. "As a magician, Merlin doesn't amount to a hill of beans. He's never learned more than a few basic tricks—pulling rabbits out of his hat, pulling nickels out of his ears. It's an embarrassment—the guy has never gone beyond doing kindergarten stuff. Excuse me for sounding mean. But he shouldn't dare to show his face around a high-class magician like myself."

At that point, I patted Clarence on his ruffle-covered shirt.

"My boy," I told him, "I'm going to stand by you as a friend. In return, you must remain loyal to me. I need you to get a message to the king."

Poor Clarence was shaking in his slippers. His mouth was hanging open.

48

"Tell the king," I said, "that I am a powerful magician. I'm the Supreme Grand High-Yu-Muck-amuck—and head of the whole tribe at that. Tell the king I'm planning a major disaster that will destroy this kingdom from top to bottom, inside and out. If I'm harmed in any way, everyone will die. Now, you'd better take this warning to the king right away."

The dear boy could barely answer me. He stumbled his way out of the cell, using the wall in order to hold himself up.

I figured it was about ten o'clock by the time Clarence left. I began to pace around and around the tiny cell. My paws left hundreds of tracks in the grime. I made myself dizzy from the constant circling, but I was too wound up to stand still. I was thinking through my plan.

At a certain point, my ears pricked up. I heard distant footsteps on the stone stairs leading down to the dungeon.

"Finally," I said, "here comes a message from the king."

The faint sound of footsteps slowly turned into thumping and clattering. It grew louder and louder. Many pairs of boots came tramping down the dark passageway.

A moment later, my cell door swung open. Six armed guards stood facing me.

Their leader spoke. "The stake is ready. Come!"

My mouth fell open. "Steak? Stake? Do you mean 'steak,' as in 'steak and a baked potato for lunch'? Or do you mean 'stake,' as in 'burn at the stake'?"

I felt stunned—like a fly that had been swatted hard. I couldn't move. The guards grabbed me. They pulled me out of the cell and dragged me along a maze of underground passageways. Finally, they carried me into the strong glare of daylight. They set me down on my four paws.

I was standing on the edge of the castle courtyard. My eyes moved immediately to the center of the area. There stood a thick, round post—the stake. To one side of it lay a tall pile of firewood. A nearby guard held a flaming torch. All around the courtyard were viewing stands. They rose up like steep bleachers surrounding a baseball field. At least four thousand people filled the stands. The king and queen sat up front on thrones.

I took in this whole scene in one second. The next second, Clarence appeared at my side. He filled me in on the news. His tongue wagged faster than a puppy's tail.

"I took your message to the king," Clarence whispered. "It frightened him to the bone. He started to give the order for your release. Then Merlin claimed your words were false. He said you did not name your disaster because you cannot produce one. He convinced the king to have you burned at the stake."

Clarence pleaded with me.

"I believe you are the greatest of all magicians. So I beg you—do not destroy the kingdom. If you must punish us for Merlin's wicked ways, make the punishment smaller. Perhaps you could cause just a short famine, or maybe a minor earthquake. I beg you!"

I took in his words and made a quick estimate: *Okay, I still have a chance to save my hide—if I play my cards perfectly.*

As the guards started to escort me to the stake, I quickly turned to Clarence. "Exactly what time is it?"

"According to the sundial," he replied, "it is ten minutes before noon."

Two minutes later, I was standing on my hind legs with my back stretched up against the stake. A hush fell over the huge crowd. The guards tied me to the stake with a heavy iron chain. Three more minutes passed. I counted out the seconds carefully in my mind. I knew my life depended on exact timing. My four legs shook.

The guards began to stack piles of firewood around my hind legs. The piles grew higher and higher. They were already up to the middle of my belly. My front legs were still free. I calculated the time: noon.

I raised my front paws straight up to the sun. I looked at the king and spoke in the loudest, deepest voice I could manage.

"I will now block out the sun. I will plunge this kingdom into the dead blackness of night forever. The fruits of the earth will rot for lack of light and warmth. The people will starve—down to the last man, woman, and child! Hear my words well!"

I was putting on a crackerjack performance. You could have heard a pin drop in that courtyard. King Arthur's handsome face turned the color of skim milk. Even my own fur stood on end.

I slowly shifted my eyes from the king up to the sun. I knew that every other pair of eyes would follow mine. I held my breath.

"Put the torch to the wood! Burn him!" someone screeched.

It was Merlin.

"I forbid it!" the king shouted.

Merlin rushed forward. The old quack was going to grab the torch himself.

I pointed one paw directly at him. "Sit down! If

51

anyone moves closer—even the king—I will blast that person with thunder and lightning!"

Merlin knew he would lose all his power at the royal court if he obeyed me. He hesitated.

There was a gasp of horror. The spectators rose to their feet—as if they were a single being. They all stared at the sun.

A rim of black shadow had crept over the edge of the brilliant disk.

I shook my paws in triumph. My ears stood straight up. My nose twitched. Yes, by golly! There it was—*my eclipse!* Ya-hoo!

I could truly see a shudder pass through the crowd. Merlin skedaddled, like a scared rabbit, back to his seat. Frightened out of their wits, the people turned to their king. They clasped their hands together. They begged the king to grant me whatever I asked in exchange for stopping the disaster.

King Arthur spoke directly to me. "Have mercy, honored sir. Name your price—any price. Take half of all my kingdom! But stop this disaster. Spare the sun. Bring it back now!"

Half the kingdom! Arthur was so shook up that he was giving away the family farm—so to speak. My fortune was made! My dish was full. If I hadn't been chained to a stake, my tail would have flapped like a flag in the wind.

I was ready to make a deal then and there. Yet I couldn't stop the eclipse. I needed to stall for time. How much time? Unfortunately, I couldn't remember exactly how long a total eclipse lasted. So I told the king I would think over his offer.

"How long, honored sir?" the king asked. "It

groweth darker by the moment. I beg of you—how long?"

I admired his self-control. He could certainly play the part of a king. He managed to be polite, even though he was shivering in his royal undershirt.

I answered him. "A half-hour . . . maybe an hour."

Pitiful cries and protests filled the air. I couldn't, however, give him a better answer. Anyway, I wanted to use the time to figure out the best bargain to make with the king.

The shadow slowly blocked out more and more of the sun. The darkness grew deeper and deeper. The crowd grew more upset. Finally, I raised a paw to get everyone's attention.

"Sir King," I said, "I have made my decision. For a lesson to you all, I will let this darkness continue. You will be plunged into the deepest darkness of night. But I will bring back the sun in its full brightness—*if* you agree to my four terms."

"Tell me your four terms," the king said.

"One . . ." I began slowly, "you will remain king of your whole kingdom. You will keep all honor and glory. Two . . . you will make me your top executive, your prime minister, for life. Three . . . you will pay me ten percent of all wealth that I create for the kingdom. Four . . . you will put into effect a cat curfew from sunset to sunrise."

"So be it!" the king declared. "Guards, set him free! I say to all my subjects—high and low, rich and poor— you must honor and obey him. He will be my right hand."

The king turned back to me.

"Now, sweep away this creeping shadow, honored

sir," the king said. "Bring back light and cheer. All my kingdom will bless you."

I, of course, had to stall for more time. The shadow hadn't even completely covered the sun yet. I said the first sensible thing that came to mind.

"It dishonors the king to have his top executive dressed so strangely," I said. "I ask for more appropriate clothes."

I hated to throw away perfectly good clothes. It was almost as bad as throwing away table scraps. Yet I knew I wouldn't gain the people's trust until I looked more like them.

"Bring him clothes fit for a prince!" the king commanded.

Some minutes later, I stood there in the courtyard unchained and stripped down to my bare fur. I was shy about that sort of thing. If it hadn't been dark outside, I would have asked to change inside.

I had chosen a good method of stalling. It took a while to put on all those sixth-century clothes. At last, I stood on my four paws, dressed like a fairytale prince. I wore a feathered hat, a long cape, a big ruffled blouse called a doublet, puffy shorts, and leather boots. I even had a sword hooked onto my belt.

The crowd was having a nervous fit in the darkness. The cold, night-like breeze made them groan with horror. Even I felt an odd shiver along my spine when the stars came out.

At last, the darkness was complete. The eclipse was total. I lifted my paws and said with loud and great seriousness, "HERDOODLESACKENFIFENMIKERSCHAFT!"

I paused for a moment to let that sink in.

Then I added, "Let the enchantment end! Let it melt away, leaving no harm to the kingdom!"

The shadow started to slip beyond the sun. A sliver of golden light appeared in the sky.

A wild cheer went up from the crowd. Men began to weep with joy. Women screamed with delight. Children who had skipped breakfast fainted from all the excitement.

Clarence, who was standing nearby, looked at me with complete love. Then he fell flat on his face—also passing out from all the excitement.

In that great moment, I made a promise. I said the following words to myself: *I will change this place. I will bring the light of knowledge and progress to the Dark Ages. I will introduce all the inventions of modern-day life. I will give these people freedom, democracy—and better food. I will offer all of them the benefits of business and profits. Here's to the Yankee attitude—and future business!*

The sliver of light continued to grow wider.

King Arthur smiled and asked me, "What name or title will you use, fair sir?"

I stroked my whiskers. It took only a moment for me to decide. I threw back my head and answered with two words.

"THE BOSS!"

Chapter Six

y life as The Boss began right away.

That very afternoon, the king had me moved into a grand apartment in the castle. My rooms were second only to his own. I had a bedroom, dining room, and living room—each the size of a large hotel lobby. The whole place almost glowed with loud-colored silk curtains. With the help of a few fluffy, silk-covered cushions, all the big oak chairs scattered around would be the perfect places for naps. The stone floors, however, had no carpets. I knew that on cold mornings I'd have to grit my teeth before putting a paw down on that icy surface.

As for conveniences—those everyday things that make life easier—we had none. There were no matches, no soap, and the reflection from the metal mirrors worked no better than a pail of water. Books? Paper? Pens? Ink? Nope. Church priests were one of the few that could read or write. Sugar? Tea? Tobacco? Nope. We didn't even have candles. Instead, we used bronze dishes filled with what looked like spoiled butter—some kind of oil. A burning rag floated in the stuff.

I didn't spend any time complaining. *Hank, I told myself, this is a grand adventure. You're like Robinson Crusoe—a shipwrecked sailor on a desert island. You'll have to put brain and paws to work. You'll have to invent, build, and organize. The sooner you get started, the better!*

I told the castle chef that I'd eat at home that evening. I invited Clarence to join me. At seven o'clock sharp, he appeared in the doorway.

"Hi-ho, my boy!" I called to him.

The sight of a familiar face made my tail wag. I trotted over to give Clarence my paw to shake. He, however, swept off his hat and bowed so low that he almost cracked his head on the hard floor.

"Fair sir," Clarence began to recite, "my lord and master, my great and—"

"Oh, hogwash and hooey!" I said. "I'm no one's lord or master."

Clarence's eyes popped open with surprise. I sat down on my haunches in front of him.

"We need to have a heart-to-heart chat," I said. "Where I come from, everyone is supposed to be free and equal. It is called a democracy. That's the kind of society I want to create here. No slaves, no nobles. No starving peasants, no fat-cat government and Church leaders. Everyone works side by side. Everyone is treated the same as everyone else. We're all digging in the same garden, so to speak. Do you follow me so far, Clarence?"

Clarence looked a little dizzy, but he managed to nod.

I went on. "You and I will work together. I'll expect you to work well. In return, I'll pay you good wages, and I'll respect you. Forget the unfair roles of servant and master—that's all twiddle-twaddle. You're an employee, and I'm your boss. Got it?"

Clarence's clear blue eyes stared deep into my brown ones. For a moment, he said nothing. Finally, a little smile tugged at the corners of his mouth. He straightened his shoulders and stood tall.

"Forsooth!" he declared. "I got it, Boss!"

My hide shivered with delight. Clarence was a great fellow and a fine student!

I pointed to the dinner table. "Sit down, my boy. Let's talk business while we eat."

We ate, and we talked—although I did most of the gabbing. I wanted to give Clarence a general idea of my plans. It was slow going, of course. Just try discussing, for example, the newspaper business with someone who had never heard of a printing press—or paper.

That night, I slept soundly. The silk sheets felt soft and smooth against my fur. The mattress had a few lumps, but it was nothing worth complaining about to the castle housekeeping staff. My dreams took me back to another time, in Hartford, Connecticut.

I dreamed I was making a telephone call to my sweetheart. I put my muzzle close to the voice transmitter. "Hello, operator," I said. I pressed the receiver under the flap of my ear. I waited to hear that pretty voice answer.

"Well, hello, Hank!" came the voice I longed to hear.

I awakened suddenly. I kept my eyes closed. I thought I was lying in my narrow bed in the room I rented in Hartford. I waited for the whistle to blow at the factory. Hartford seemed real to me. Camelot seemed like a dream.

I opened my eyes. To my surprise, I saw the silk curtains, the stone floor, my silver water dish. I sat up and pressed my furred spine into the soft pillows. A young page entered the room with a basin of warm water. He began to wash my muzzle with a damp cloth.

"Gad-zooks!" I whispered. "Camelot *is* real."

So it went every morning for several months. Then, gradually, the dream of Hartford faded. My mind accepted that I was living in the sixth century. I began to feel as much at home in King Arthur's court as I had in nineteenth-century Connecticut.

Of course, I missed my sweetheart more than a little. Her "Hello, Hank!" would have made my fur ripple with joy. So, now and then, I gave myself a pep talk: *Hank, sniff out the good stuff wherever you are. Prick up your ears to hear the best in life. And remember—with hard work, the food will improve.*

Seven years went by quickly. Time always flew by when your wits, as well as all four legs, were working hard. I had set a big goal for myself: to change the Dark Ages. At the end of seven years, I must say that my progress impressed even me.

I had planted the ideas of nineteenth-century civilization right smack-dab in the middle of the sixth century. Hidden away in the countryside, I had schools, factories, and laboratories of every type. I set up military academies and docks for shipbuilding. I gathered together the best minds I could find and trained them in all sorts of jobs. My assistants traveled all over the kingdom, looking for new talent.

No one could go near my factories and schools without a special permit. I had to keep all my projects secret from the two main forces that did not want to see progress come: the powerful noble class, and the Church. England had no freedom of religion; people could not worship in any way they chose. There was one official Church. The Church had as much power and wealth as the nobles did. My modern democratic society would put an end to all those special privileges that benefit only a small group.

So this was my plan: I would introduce my changes bit by bit over a long period of time. Then, when I finally had enough people agreeing with the new ways I was changing the kingdom—*ta-da!* I'd reveal all my hidden inventions—and sweep away the Dark Ages.

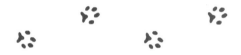

Early one summer morning, I was thinking about my project as I sat on a chair in my bedroom. I heard three quick taps on the door.

"Come in, Clarence," I called out, recognizing Clarence's knock.

The door opened, and Clarence walked in. He was now twenty-two years old. He was also the finest young man on earth, as far as I was concerned. He was my top executive. I admired him as a coworker. I also loved him as if we'd been brothers.

I showed Clarence a container of flea powder. "Fresh from the lab," I said. "I don't know if it works yet, but it sure smells better than the last batch."

Clarence sat down on a chair near mine. He sniffed the flea powder. "Smells jim-dandy Boss." He rubbed some on his neck.

Clarence spoke Yankee English almost as well as he spoke the sixth-century kind.

"Boss, you'd better hurry up and finish getting dressed," he said. "You don't want to be late again for the jousting tournament."

I sighed. My tail stopped wagging. I loved a good sports event as much as anyone. Yet, just the mention of the tournaments—those contests between knights on horseback—would make me lose my appetite.

Picture this: Two grown men riding toward each other as fast as they can. Each tries to knock the other off his horse. Then they fight each other with swords, trying to hack off each other's arms and legs. Dozens of knights and horses get hurt every week. Some of them even die. And they call this a sport? What violence! What a waste of talent and energy!

"Let's go, Boss," Clarence said.

He tossed my cape and hat to me. I nodded. I swung the garment over my shoulders. Then I put on my hat.

I went to the tournaments for two reasons. First, I wanted everyone to think of me a regular member of the community. Second, if I studied the tournaments, I might figure out how to replace them with a more healthy sport—like baseball. I could just imagine a team of my own . . . the Yankees.

Clarence and I left the castle and hurried down a hill to a flat, grassy area nearby. We took our places in one of the huge viewing stands set up for the occasion. These tall wooden bleachers were decorated with dozens of silk banners and curtains. We had front-row seats, next to the king and queen's cushioned chairs. I lifted my hat to them as I settled in.

The viewing stand overlooked a dirt playing field

called the list. This was as long as two city blocks, and as wide as a broad boulevard. At one end, I saw Sir Sagramore, an especially brutal knight. He sat on his horse, in full armor. At the other end of the list, Sir Launcelot sat on his horse. He, too, was in full armor.

I whispered to Clarence, "If I were the betting kind, I'd put my money on Launcelot."

"Who wouldn't?" Clarence whispered in reply. "But Sir Sagramore hath courage and a most foul temper. He won't go down like a dead balloon."

"You mean a *lead* balloon," I whispered.

A long trumpet blast announced the start of the first joust. Sir Sagramore and Sir Launcelot lowered the visors of their metal helmets. They pointed their long spears at each other.

All eyes turned to Queen Guenever. She stood and raised one graceful arm over the list. She held a white-satin handkerchief. She smiled at Sir Launcelot, who was her favorite knight. Then she let the handkerchief drop. The instant it touched the ground—*wham!*—the action began.

The two knights kicked their horses. The animals sprang forward. They galloped toward each other at full speed. The horses used in jousts were specially bred for size and strength. The knights lowered their heads to their horses' necks. They rode closer, closer, and still even closer. The moment they came within striking range—*crack!* They bashed their spears against each other. Both spears broke, the pieces falling to the ground.

"Ouch!" I closed my eyes for an instant.

When I opened my eyes, Launcelot and Sagramore were still wobbling in their saddles. Neither fell off his horse. They turned their animals around. Each galloped to his end of the list. Servants handed each competitor a long, heavy sword. Then, once again, they came charging toward each other.

Slam! Thwack! Sword against sword. *Bam! Clang!* Sword against armor. The horses moved closer and closer to the viewing stands. The knights were fighting right in front of us. The crowd jumped up and down. They cheered. The most awful bangs and whacks made them cheer even louder.

The all-out violence made my whiskers quiver. I mumbled a short prayer for Sir Launcelot and his horse, both of whom I liked.

Smack! Sir Launcelot delivered one doozy of a blow to the middle of Sir Sagramore's back. *Crash!* Sir Sagramore toppled against the viewing stand just in front of me. He grabbed the railing and clung to it like a huge metal spider.

Just then, Merlin pushed his way past me. That old pain in the neck was always in the wrong place at the wrong time. He was waving his silly magic wand and nearly poked out one of my eyes.

"Go away!" I said under my breath. "If you're gonna hang around like a pesky fly, do it in front of someone else!"

As bad luck would have it, Sir Sagramore thought I was talking to him. His eyes looked angrily through the slits in his visor. For a moment, he stopped concentrating on the joust. His grip on the railing slipped. He fell to the ground.

Sir Launcelot seized the opportunity. He leaned over on his horse and pinned Sir Sagramore to the ground with his sword.

"Do ye yield, Sir Sagramore?" Launcelot shouted.

Sir Sagramore had no other choice. In an angry voice, he answered, "I yield!"

The crowd screamed and clapped. Queen Guenever nearly fainted with happiness.

Clarence turned to me. "You're in big trouble now, Boss."

"You can say that again," I answered.

Clarence nodded. "You're in big trouble now, Boss."

I watched Sir Sagramore. A servant was helping him get to his feet. His armor clanked and banged like a broken stovepipe. As soon as he was standing upright, he flipped open his visor. He turned to me. His face was as red as a boiled beet.

I knew what was coming. My fur bristled.

Sir Sagramore pulled off one of his metal gloves. Looking me straight in the eye, he threw the glove to the ground. That meant he was about to challenge me to a fight.

"Sir Boss!" he called out. "Ye did insult my person and my honor with rude words. Therefore, I answer you with a challenge. I say we shall meet on this same list and joust! I will nameth a future date. What sayeth you, Sir Boss?"

I know it was useless to argue with a knight—especially Sir Sagramore—once he had a bee in his bonnet. I also knew I'd have to win the joust—or lose my reputation. I accepted my fate. I answered in the most serious voice I could manage. "Sir Sagramore, knight of the Round Table—I, The Boss, accept your challenge!"

Well, forsooth! Hank Morgan faces a challenge that's both unexpected and unwanted. He must joust like a sixth-century knight.

Back in Oakdale, Joe and David face a challenge that they have created themselves. Using cutting-edge technology, they jump right into the newsletter business.

Chapter Seven

"Wow! Look at this, Joe!"

David pointed to his computer screen. He and Joe were sitting at the large desk in David's bedroom. It was late Saturday afternoon. They'd been working on their newsletter all day. David had just designed a masthead—the newsletter's name as it would appear at the top of the front page.

Before Joe got a chance to look at the screen, David thumped his fists on the desk. "This is going to be good. I mean, really good!" He tipped back his chair. "I am really glad we decided to report on all the sports. It's a completely new newsletter. Six pages! We can pass this issue out on Monday. Then it'll be a snap to put out a special one-sheet extra edition about Thursday's soccer playoff."

"This newsletter is a whole new ballgame," Joe said. "New and improved. Bigger and better." He gave David's shoulder a playful shove.

Wishbone tried to see the screen from where he was standing on the floor. "Let me see, guys. You know,

spectators down here in the cheap seats have viewing rights, too."

David moved to the side so that Joe could see the bold lettering:

The CHAMP
Inside Sequoyah Sports

Joe nodded. "I like it. Great name. Great look. Let's go with it."

Wishbone agreed. "Yes, it's short, sweet, and packs a punch—like someone I know. Speaking of whom—what about *my* column, guys? I feel I have a lot to offer this publication—brains, talent, wit, four paws, washable fur coat . . ."

Wishbone's ears pricked up.

"Hark! Familiar footsteps in the hallway. Here comes Sam."

A moment later, the bedroom door opened. Sam stepped inside. "Hi, guys. I can't believe you're still at work. You haven't budged since I stopped by right after breakfast this morning."

"Actually, I insisted on a lunch break," Wishbone said. "It's guaranteed in my pet contract."

Joe motioned for Sam to come closer. "Wait till you see everything we've done. You're in for one big surprise."

David gathered up papers that were lying on the desk. "Take a look at these." He handed the sheets to Sam, one at a time. "Here's our first editorial. It's about school spirit and the reason for the newsletter. Then, here's an article about the very first American football games. We found really neat illustrations to go with it. Then we have an interview I did on the phone with the captain of the girls' hockey team. She's going to drop off some photos that her mom took at the last game."

"Here's the article I wrote," Joe said. "It's about Sequoyah's chances in the soccer playoffs. We're publishing season statistics for all the teams. I also did a joke column called 'Sport Jester.'"

Wishbone barked. "Get it, Sam? It's a play on words—'court jester.' Kings and queens used to have entertainers called court jesters. It was their job to make the royal household laugh. Sounds like a job I might have liked a few hundred years ago. But today I'm aiming at a newspaper career. How about putting in a good word for me?"

Sam sat down on the bed and shuffled through the sheets of paper. She looked completely puzzled. "I don't get it. I thought you were doing the design for a report on the big soccer game. This looks like a whole new sports newsletter."

"That's *exactly* what it is," David said to her. "We'll

be passing it out at school on Monday—the day after tomorrow."

"When we started working," Joe added, "we got so many great ideas. They were just too good to drop. It seemed like a waste not to cover the other sports. We'll do the report on Thursday's soccer game as a separate feature story. We'll pass it out on Friday."

David grinned. "This is really going to impress everyone on Monday. Just wait until Anna Valdez and Ryan Clark see this. I'll bet they never even dreamed of a newsletter like this."

Sam looked up. Her expression had changed from very confused to very worried. "I was wondering about that. Do you think Anna and Ryan might be . . . insulted?"

David looked puzzled. "Why? They want the school to have a sports newsletter more than anyone else. They'll be really happy to see such a good one. It's progress!"

"It'll be an amazing surprise," Joe said. "That's part of the fun—for us and for everyone else."

Wishbone gave his head a quick scratch with a back paw. *I wonder what Sam's got on her mind. She's always so quick, smart, and sensitive. She reminds me of . . . me.*

"I'm scanning a terrific cartoon into the computer," David said. "It'll be done in a minute. You'll love this, Sam."

Sam shook her head. "I'd like to see it, but I've got to get home." She put the pile of papers on the desk and walked to the bedroom door.

David and Joe were huddled over the computer.

"Well, your newsletter does look great," Sam said. "So . . . good luck at school on Monday. 'Bye."

Joe raised a hand to wave. David murmured, "See ya." Their eyes remained fixed on the glowing screen.

Talk about being determined! Joe and David have set themselves a goal. They won't let anything distract them from reaching it. I haven't seen such focus, such eagerness, such devotion since . . . the last time I ate.

Hank Morgan works in exactly the same way. When he has a job to do, he doesn't want to think about anything else. Sometimes, however, events slip out of his control.

Chapter Eight

The morning after Sir Sagramore challenged me to a joust, I went to my castle office. I hopped onto my desk chair.

Hank, I said to myself, *you have work to do. Don't ruffle your fur about the joust until Sir Sagramore names a date.*

A minute later, my mind was buzzing with my latest idea for improving the sixth century: personal cleanliness. I had plans for a major campaign—complete with slogans. My assistants would travel across the kingdom. They'd sell whiz-bang new products door-to-door: soap, toothpaste, deodorant, nail clippers, and, of course, flea powder. I had created a few nifty slogans to use in my ad campaign:

You scream. I scream. We all scream for hygiene!

A knight with clean feet can't be beat!

While deep in thought, I heard familiar footsteps in the hallway.

"Come on in, Clarence," I called.

As the door opened, I picked up a small tube with my teeth. I waved it at Clarence as he hurried toward me.

"New tufpaste sampo!" I said. "New tufpaste sampo!"

Clarence pulled the tube out of my mouth.

"New toothpaste sample!" I repeated. "It's mint-flavored."

Clarence tossed the tube onto the desk. "Boss, something much more important—"

My ears stood straight up. "More important? Clarence, a civilization that doesn't know anything about personal hygiene—health and good grooming—is a civilization that stinks in more ways than one."

Clarence didn't even hear me. He was so excited he couldn't stand still.

"Boss, you're going on a quest—a search—for adventure! You're leaving this afternoon!"

I loved the idea—for the first few seconds.

"'Adventure' is my middle name!" I said. "Climb a mountain. Stare down a bear. Dig for gold. Count me in, partner!" Then I remembered—"Uh . . . do you mean a sixth-century quest for adventure?" I was immediately on my guard. "You mean roam around, looking for dragons to slay, and enchanted princesses to rescue?" I shook my head. "I've got better things to do."

Clarence grabbed a chair near mine and sat down. He leaned forward until our noses nearly touched. News gushed out of him like oil out of a Texas well.

Sir Sagramore was setting off to search for the Holy Grail. According to legend, the Grail was the cup that Jesus Christ used at the Last Supper. It had been lost for hundreds of years. All the knights took a turn at Grail-hunting now and then. As far as I was concerned, none of them would know a Grail if he tripped over it. No matter—they got points just for roaming around for years.

Anyway, Sir Sagramore had announced that he and I would joust when he got back. Meanwhile, King Arthur decided I needed to have some knightlike adventures. Then I would be worthy of fighting Sir Sagramore. That morning, someone had brought the king news of a quest opportunity. He was offering it to me.

I rubbed the fur on my forehead. I had a headache already.

"So what's the quest? What am I searching for?" I asked Clarence. "I'll bet I must travel to a faraway land to rescue twelve princesses held captive by a giant with four arms."

Clarence smiled. "It's thirty-six princesses this time. And there are three giants, each with a huge eye in the middle of his forehead."

Clarence grasped my shoulder. He stopped smiling.

"Boss, I know it's all chuckle-head nonsense. But the king is showing his favor—admiration of you—by granting you this quest. Every knight of the Round Table was begging him for it. You can't refuse the king. Just ride around the countryside for a while and come back with a few prisoners. I'll watch over everything while you're gone."

I sighed. This quest appealed to me about as much as getting my tail caught in a lawn mower. Yet I knew everything Clarence said was true. I could not refuse such an offer—no matter how daffy it was—if it came directly from the king.

Right after lunch, Clarence, Sir Launcelot, and a few other knights helped me put on my armor.

First, they wrapped me in a layer of blankets. This was supposed to act as a cushion and also keep the cold metal off my sensitive hide. Next, I put on a chain-mail shirt. Chain mail was a flexible material made of tiny pieces of metal, all linked together. It weighed a ton. Next, I stuck my back paws into metal shoes—flat boats topped with bands of iron. After that came iron shields for my hind legs, a breastplate, and a back plate.

That much armor was already dragging me down like an anchor. Yet, we hadn't finished by a long shot. The knights strapped me into a kind of skirt made of broad iron bands. It hung shorter in the back so I could sit on my horse. Next, they belted on my sword. After that, they put protective iron pipes around my front legs. Finally, they shoved my head into the iron rat trap they called a helmet.

"Holy mackerel!" I said. "I feel like I'm wearing a portable jail. I wouldn't put my worst enemy in one of these suits. Well, on second thought . . ."

No one was listening. The knights carried me to my horse as if they were carrying a dead body into a funeral parlor.

Clank, clank, clunk. They sat me upright on my steed. Sir Launcelot thrust my spear into a holder on the saddle. Clarence reached up and hung a large shield around my neck. He raised my visor so I could take a semi-normal breath. That's when I noticed her.

A young noblewoman stood to one side of my horse. She bowed, her slim figure dipping gracefully. Her long, light brown curls bounced up and down. Her gray eyes twinkled. As she spoke, she showed no shyness, and a dimple appeared in her chin.

"Fair lord, Sir Boss, I am ready to ride."

I looked down at Clarence. "She's ready to *what?*"

Clarence replied in a whisper. "She's the one who brought the king news of the captive princesses. She asked the king for help. She'll guide you to the castle where the princesses are being kept. You'll protect her during your travels."

First, I was flabbergasted. Next, I panicked. No one had ever mentioned this part of the deal to me. Roam around the kingdom with an unknown young lady on my horse? Good golly! I hadn't even met her parents. And what about protecting her properly? I couldn't even wag my tail or flash my teeth underneath all that armor.

I was too surprised to speak for a moment. Then it was too late. The knights lifted the young lady onto a cushion that they had placed just behind my saddle. She also needed something to hold on to. She grabbed a fistful of my chain-mail shirt.

The whole royal court gathered to see us off. Trumpets blared. Banners waved. Everyone cheered.

I spurred my horse on. Off we went.

"Farewell! God be with you! Good luck!"

I took one last look at Clarence. He raised two fists—thumbs up. I groaned.

For the next hour, my horse trotted at a brisk pace through meadows and woods. The clanking armor made such a racket that I was sorry I had such sensitive ears. My visor slammed shut. Gradually, I felt less embarrassed by my awkward situation, so I could speak to my companion.

"May I ask what your name is?"

"I am the Demoiselle Alisande la Carteloise, may it please you, fair sir," she said.

"Well, it doesn't exactly *dis*please me," I said. "But I'd prefer something shorter. How about . . . Sandy?"

"As you wish, fair sir," she replied.

She seemed nice enough. I decided to get down to business.

"Now, Sandy," I said, "exactly where is this castle with the thirty-six captured princesses and the one-eyed giants?"

"Ah, as to that," she said, "it lieth in a far-off country. Forsooth, it is so very many miles and—"

"How many miles?" I asked.

"Ah, fair sir," she said, "it were overly hard to tell. For they are so many miles, and they do so lap the one mile upon the other, one may not know the one mile from its fellow. Ye wit—"

"Okay, chuck the miles," I said. "What direction is the castle from here?"

Off she went again. "Ah, please you, sir—it hath no direction from here. By reason that the road lieth not straight, but it turneth evermore. Wherefore . . ."

I stopped listening. I couldn't pull facts out of that woman with a steam-powered pump. I'd have to blast them out with dynamite—which I hadn't brought along.

There's only one thing to do, I told myself. *Keep riding, and let the one-eyed giants find us.*

We rode on. Sandy chattered on. I began to notice new problems. The summer sun was heating up my metal armor. I might as well have been wearing a stove. Moisture from my breath condensed inside my helmet. It drenched my fur. It dripped down my forehead and into my eyes. I, of course, couldn't wipe it away. I couldn't move. Besides, I had stuffed my handkerchief into my helmet, along with a few other basic necessities, such as my pipe and a snack. Where else could I put them? A suit of armor does not have pockets.

We crossed a dry field. The horse kicked up clouds of dust. The dust went up my nose.

A-a-a-choo! *A-choo!*

My nose was running. I couldn't imagine being more uncomfortable. Foolish little ol' me. Cooped up in that armor for so long, I began to itch. First, my belly, then my rump. Soon my entire body—from muzzle to tail—was itching like crazy. Think about it. I was inside; my paws were outside; a layer of iron separated us.

Just when I thought I could stand no more discomfort, a fly flew through the slits in my visor. It landed on my nose. I tried to shake it out of my helmet. That was a total bust. The fly flitted from nose to ear flap to the side of my muzzle. It buzzed and bit the whole way.

I reached my boiling point.

"Hang the man who invented armor!" I yelled. "Or, better yet, burn him at the stake!"

Sandy suddenly stopped talking. After a moment's quiet, she murmured, "Ah, me thinks Sir Boss doth need rest and water. Let us stop by yonder stream."

I quickly got the horse down to the edge of the stream. Then Sandy took charge. She got off the steed. She helped me half-slide and half-fall to the ground. She pulled off my helmet, unloaded what I had packed in there, and filled the thing with water. I lowered my muzzle into that cool wetness and drank . . . and drank . . . and drank.

Next, Sandy had me stand on my hind legs, with my front legs stretched up against a tree. She poured water down the neck opening of my armor. Oh, heavenly relief! Oh, divine comfort! Oh, precious lady of the water! She poured again and again until I was happily soaked. I didn't care a bit if my armor rusted.

78

"Sandy," I gasped, "you have the makings of Yankee genius!"

We settled ourselves in the shade of a large elm tree. I gave Sandy one of the sandwiches I had packed in my helmet. She didn't know what to do with it. As soon as I took a bite of mine, however, she followed my example.

"Ah," she said after the first swallow, "'tis goodly of taste. 'Tis most new to my tongue. Perchance, Sir Boss, know you the name of such a taste?"

I nodded as I licked my muzzle. "Egg salad on rye."

After our snack, I found my homemade pipe. I'd also packed some matches from a new factory, and dried willow bark for tobacco. I tapped some willow bark into the bowl of the pipe with my paw. I took a match and struck it against one of my shoes, and lit the pipe. I puffed long and deep.

When the first cloud of smoke escaped from my mouth, Sandy shrieked. "Aaahh! Heaven protect me! You are a dragon!"

After that outburst, she flopped over in a dead faint. I emptied a helmetful of water over her head. She sat up and started to shriek again. I quickly put out my pipe. It took me a good fifteen minutes to calm her down. I did my best to explain the meaning of *pipe* and *tobacco*. At the end of my efforts, she turned up her nose.

"Me thinks it a nasty and smelly habit," she said. "And bad for one's health, too. I beg you, Sir Boss, not to blow smoke in my presence."

Being a gentleman, I gave her my promise. She wrapped up my pipe, tobacco, and matches in her long scarf.

As soon as Sandy helped me squeeze my head back into my helmet, we set off. This time, however, I had to walk on all fours while she rode. Like any knight weighed down by heavy armor, I needed at least two strong men to lift me onto my horse.

We started to cross an enormous field of grass. I lost myself in thoughts of my cleanliness campaign. Cool peppermint mouthwash, cool spearmint toothpaste, cool menthol flea powder, cool—

Sandy gasped and cried, "Defend thyself, Sir Boss! Threat to life comes your way!"

I looked up. A dozen armed knights stood on the far side of the field. Their horses were resting under some nearby trees. The instant the knights noticed me, they raised their spears and rushed to mount their horses. I was in for a good fight—twelve against one.

I reviewed my options. I didn't have many.

I turned to Sandy. "Quick! My pipe and tobacco—give them to me!"

Sandy understood my plan at once. She stuffed some tobacco into the pipe and handed it to me. Then she lit a match by striking it across the bottom of her shoe.

The knights were on their horses. As Sandy and I tried desperately to light my pipe, the knights started to gallop toward us. They rushed forward like an ocean wave. Holding the pipe steady, I inhaled as hard and fast as I could.

The knights came straight at us. When I could see the whites of the horses' eyes, I flipped down my visor. The thundering sound of hooves made my ears throb. With every muscle of my mouth, throat, and muzzle, I exhaled. White smoke blew out through the slits in my visor.

The knights screamed. Their horses reared up. The

single wave of warriors shattered into a dozen pieces. Barely able to control their horses, the men turned and retreated at top speed.

When the knights had gone about two hundred yards, they stopped. They stared at Sandy and me. They waited.

I waved to Sandy. "You'd better get out of here while you can. They'll probably charge again. I'm not sure I can stop them a second time."

"Nay, Sir Boss," Sandy said. She sounded quite cheerful. "Yonder knights have had their fill. They wait to yield to you. They are too afraid to come closer. I will go to them."

She rode straight over to them. After two minutes of conversation, the knights bowed their heads and galloped off.

"What's the deal?" I asked as soon as Sandy rode back.

"I did tell them you are The Boss," she explained. "This struck them sore with fear and dread. Now they ride to Camelot. They will yield to you at the royal court. Henceforth, they are your soldiers and will follow your command."

I sat back on my haunches and looked at the young woman. My tail wagged with admiration.

"Sandy, you are a daisy!" I declared. "Thanks to you, I've got my required adventure points. I can forget the princesses now and get back to work. So . . . I guess it's time to say good-bye."

Sandy shook her head firmly. "Good-bye, nay. I may not leave my knight, my champion, my hero. I shall stayeth with him until some other knight may defeat him in battle."

Her knight! I swallowed hard. My hide suddenly felt prickly. It was like an allergy attack. My voice squeaked. "Uh . . . Sandy, I think I'm the loner type—you know, lone wolf, stray dog, odd duck—"

Sandy shook her head calmly. "Me thinks a lady knoweth her knight."

I knew I was beat. I turned the horse toward Camelot.

Chapter Nine

Sandy and I made our way back to the castle. I immediately sent my twelve captured knights to rescue the princesses. It was the perfect job to keep them busy and out of my fur for a few years. I made Sandy the manager of my start-up, top-secret telephone and telegraph system. She took to the communications business like a duck to water. Meanwhile, Sir Sagramore left town for the Grail hunt. No one knew when he'd pop up again.

In late October, several months after my return to Camelot, I spoke to King Arthur about a new plan.

"Your Majesty," I said, "I need to study the life of the ordinary people. I want to know their customs. I'm going to wander around the kingdom for a few weeks, dressed as a freeman."

In sixth-century England, the population was divided into four groups: the powerful nobles, the powerful Church officials, the pitiful slaves, and the almost-as-pitiful freemen. The freemen included peasant farmers and craftsmen such as carpenters and blacksmiths.

King Arthur's face lit up like a brand-new electric lamp.

"Forsooth, 'tis a wonderful idea!" he exclaimed. "I will go with you! I will tell the court we are off to hunt deer."

I knew the king would be as helpful as a bad toothache on my voyage. Although I liked him, he reminded me of a pretty picture: fine to look at, but nothing solid beneath the surface. Yet I certainly couldn't forbid him to come along. I set my mind and paws to the job of getting us ready. I put Clarence in charge of my regular projects. Sandy would help him out.

I found plain robes of rough, brown-linen cloth for the king and me. The king's robe hung straight down from his neck to his ankles. Mine stopped just short of my tail.

Like all nobles, King Arthur wore his hair long. Clarence helped me cut it. We put a bowl over the king's head and chopped off whatever hung below the rim. We also cut off most of his long, thick beard. When I stepped back to admire our handiwork, my jaw popped open like a trapdoor. The most handsome man in England now looked as rough and plain as his subjects!

The next morning before dawn, the king and I slipped out of the castle unseen. I carried a small pack on my back. It held a few basic supplies.

By the time the sun was shining high in the sky, we had walked about ten miles. We tramped along a dirt path that led us through fields and woods. We saw few huts and few people. I thanked my lucky stars for this because we already had a big problem. The king walked like a king.

"Your Majesty," I said, "it's not enough to dress like a freeman. You must walk, talk, and behave like one. If you don't, the ordinary people will never trust us. The knights will beat you to a pulp for not acting common enough."

The king thought about this and finally nodded. "That is wisdom I may not deny. Tell me what to do. I will try my best."

"Let's try some play-acting," I suggested. I sat down on my haunches by the side of the path. "Okay, here's the scene. You are farmer Jones. You're tired, poor, hungry, sick, and your prize-winning cow just died. Now—walk along the path in front of me."

The king considered what I'd said and started to walk.

"No, no, no!" I called out. I thumped my tail. "Look at you—spine straight, head high, shoulders back. That's awful! You've got to droop like a cooked noodle, wobble like jelly. Sag for me, Jones! Stagger and stumble, man!"

King Arthur tried walking again. This time he looked like a king with a bad back and trick knee. I groaned, lay down, and covered my head.

We practiced for the rest of the morning, and most of the afternoon. We paused only for a snack. The king made a little progress—very little. He had as much acting talent as a doorknob. My paws began to itch to move on. I decided to risk a test. We would visit the next peasant hut that we saw.

Two miles down the path, we came to a shabby hut. The nearby fields had been stripped of their crops. We saw no animals—or any other living thing. A terrible stillness hung over the place.

As I walked up to the door, a shiver ran along my spine and ruffled my fur. I knocked. No one answered. I pushed the door open slowly.

My nose instantly picked up a foul smell. My eyes made out some dim forms in the dark hut. As the king and I stepped inside, someone lying on the floor—a woman—moaned.

"Have mercy!" she cried. "The noble lord and the Church officials have already taken everything. Nothing is left!"

"We haven't come to steal, poor woman," I said. "We are honest strangers in this land."

The woman gasped. "Then flee! For fear of God, flee! This place is under God's curse and the curse of the Church!"

My eyes had become used to the dim light. I could see how thin the woman was. She stared at me with hollowed-out eyes.

"I don't care about the Church's curse," I said. "I want to help you."

Tall and as graceful as ever, the king moved closer to the woman. I was surprised to see him stretch out his hand to her in sympathy and concern.

"Bless you, bless you!" the woman whispered. "God grant me a sip of water—"

I saw a bowl lying on the floor. I grabbed it by the rim with my teeth. I dashed outside, to a stream that flowed near the hut. Moving as quickly as I could, I returned with a bowlful of water.

The king was pulling open the shutters that covered the window opening to let in some fresh air. As the woman reached for the bowl of water, light from the window fell on her face.

Smallpox!

My fur stood on end. I whirled around and spoke to the king. "Leave, sire! Out the door with you now! This woman is dying of the disease that killed hundreds in the town of London. I'm not at risk—I had smallpox when I was younger. But this hut is truly a deathtrap for you. Go!"

King Arthur did not budge. "I will remain and help," he said calmly. "It would be shameful for me to withdraw my hand when help is needed." With great dignity, he stepped toward the woman.

I shook my head violently. This decision might cost the king his life. Yet I knew that I couldn't argue with him. Sympathy and a sense of duty moved him to take action.

The dying woman spoke in a hoarse whisper. "Oh, kind friends, will ye climb the ladder to the loft? Tell me what ye find there."

I turned toward the ladder. The king, however, brushed past me. As he started to climb, he noticed a man lying in the corner.

"Is that your husband?" the king asked the woman quietly.

"Yes," she said. "God be blessed—he suffers no more. He died an hour ago."

A minute later, I heard a noise. The king was climbing down from the loft. Against his chest he held a slender girl of about ten years of age. She, too, was dying of smallpox.

I looked at the king and thought, *I'm witnessing the highest form of bravery in this hut. King Arthur is challenging death, unarmed. The odds are against him. He can't win a prize here or listen to an audience applaud. Only generosity and human kindness make him act.*

In that moment, I saw for the first time that Arthur had true nobility and dignity. He was more than a pretty picture.

The king gently laid the girl next to her mother. The dying woman kissed her daughter and whispered loving words to her. A faint light of response flickered in the child's eyes.

While the woman continued to lovingly caress her child, she told us her story.

"Like all peasants," she said, "we rent our land from the local nobleman. One day, he found three of his fruit trees cut down. He accused my three innocent sons of the crime. He threw them into his castle's dungeon. There they will stay until they die.

"When harvest time came, my husband and I had to gather the noble's crops before we picked our own. We could not work fast enough. We never had time to work in our own fields. This angered the nobleman and the Church, because we must give them part of our own crop. To punish us, they took everything—crops, animals, tools, furniture.

"Ten days ago, I became ill. My husband and daughter caught the disease. In my grief, I spoke angry words against the Church and the nobleman. The Church officials found out. They put their curse on our family. No one may come near us. We are left here to die alone."

Every bit of my fur trembled with pity. Every muscle beneath my hide shook with anger. I looked at King Arthur. Tears of compassion were running down his face.

At midnight, all had ended. The king and I found a few rags to cover the mother, father, and child. No one would be allowed to give them a proper burial. The little hut would be their grave.

King Arthur and I returned to the dirt path. We walked for more than an hour in the dark without speaking. At last, we lay down in the damp grass to sleep. The night passed, dark and silent.

Shortly after dawn, we awoke.

"We need to clear our minds," I said to the king. "I suggest a bath in the brook over there."

"Wet my person? Have you lost your wits?!" the king exclaimed. "A bath will certainly kill ye. Damp the head, dead in bed!"

I decided to ignore this sixth-century gem of wisdom.

I trotted down to the brook and wiggled out of my robe. I gripped a bar of my newly created soap and leaped into the refreshing water. I worked the soap into a thick lather. Then I rubbed it deep into my fur. Ah, pure pleasure! I thought about my cleanliness campaign. I couldn't help but sing: "Hank with clean feet feels really neat!"

Two minutes of fast doggie-paddling rinsed me clean. Back on the bank, I did an all-over shake. Water sprayed off my fur in every direction.

The king stared at me in horror. "If ye survive this, ye are truly the greatest magician of all times."

As soon as I was dressed, we started to walk down the path. An hour or so later, a distant noise made my ears prick up.

"A large group on horseback is coming toward us," I said.

The king looked impressed. "Your powers to predict the future amaze me."

A few minutes later, twenty men on horseback came trotting down the path. A noble wrapped in a velvet cloak led the group. Armed men and servants rode behind him.

I glanced at King Arthur. He stood tall and stately, like a marble statue.

"Bow your head, sire!" I whispered. "Act like a peasant."

It was too late. The noble had seen us. He frowned and reigned in his horse.

"Rude piece of dirt!" he said to the king. He raised his whip, then stopped his arm in midair. "Who are you?" he demanded to know.

I jumped in front of the king. I stretched out my front legs and bowed low.

"Noble sir," I said, "we are peaceful strangers. We come from a faraway country on business. We know no one in this land."

The noble asked a dozen more questions. I answered with great respect. Yet I didn't reveal any information about our true identities. I said we planned to continue down the same road.

The noble stared hard at us. I didn't like the look in his eyes. He seemed to be planning something. After a few minutes, he turned to a servant.

"Bring forward two horses," he ordered. "Let these two travelers climb onto them."

The servant did as he was told.

Next the noble spoke to the king and me. "I travel this road to the town called Cambenet. It is a journey of twenty miles. You can ride with us that far."

We could not refuse a noble's offer. I thanked him with the necessary humble manner. Meanwhile, the fur on the back of my neck bristled. That was a sure sign something was wrong. Why would a noble show any sort of kindness to two lowly freemen?

We stopped at an inn to eat. During that time, I learned the noble's name—Lord Grip. His great estate was a day's journey beyond Cambenet.

In mid-afternoon, we reached the town. A crowd had gathered in the market square. We all got down from our horses. I thanked Lord Grip again for his favor.

"Let's see what's going on in that crowd," I suggested to King Arthur.

We walked across the square. I had to push my way through a forest of legs until I had a clear view. What I saw sickened me.

"A slave auction!" I cried. "People are sold like a bunch of hogs to whomever will pay the highest price."

The slaves—men, women, and children—huddled together on the ground. They were tired, weak, wasted, and physically abused. Iron chains ran from the leather belts around their waists to the iron cuffs around their wrists and ankles. Still more chains bound one slave to another. The iron had bruised their skin, making sores that were badly infected. Walking for hundreds of miles had torn up their feet. Underneath the few rags they wore, we could see whip slashes on their skin. The slaves stared blankly at the ground. Except for the awful clanking of chains, the slaves made no sounds.

Anger boiled up within me. Blood rushed to my head. My forehead throbbed. The muscles of my muzzle ached with tension. I could stand it no longer.

"In the name of—" I shouted. "Aaahh-ooof!"

Four of Lord Grip's servants pulled my legs out from under me. *Clank-click! Clank-click!* The men snapped heavy iron cuffs around my legs. They locked an iron collar around my neck. I struggled to get free. *Thud!* A heavy boot slammed into my ribs.

I twisted back and forth wildly. What had happened to the king? Then I saw him less than six feet from me. He, too, was in iron cuffs.

The king roared at Lord Grip, who stood nearby. "What do you mean by this wicked jest?"

The nobleman paid no attention to King Arthur. He nodded to a servant and said coolly, "Sell these two slaves."

Chapter Ten

"Slaves!" King Arthur's deep voice shook with rage. "I am Ar——"

Lord Grip grasped his whip and raised it high.

Crack! The whip slashed across the king's chest. *Crack!* It snapped across his face.

King Arthur froze. I knew such violent treatment shocked his royal being, but he did not even flinch. What a noble spirit! I had to admire him. His shoulders remained straight, his head high. He started to raise a fist. Lord Grip's servants pulled the king to the ground. I managed to get close enough to whisper in his ear.

"Sire, do not try to fight them now. We'll have to wiggle out of this tight spot together." I tried to encourage him. "I'll have us both free in less time than it takes for a dog to bury a bone."

My prediction missed the mark—by a lot. In less time than it takes for a dog to bury a bone, Lord Grip had sold us to a slave dealer. Our new master chained us to the end of his long line of two dozen other slaves. With a whip cracking over our heads and a heavy wooden club jabbing into our ribs, we marched out of Cambenet.

The king glared at me. His eyes flashed with anger. Was he furious because we'd been sold as slaves? No, siree. He was all bent out of shape because the slave dealer had bought him for a measly seven dollars. I, however, cost nine.

This fact pricked the king like a thorn bush. It got under his skin, plucked his whiskers, and stepped on his toes until he just about drove me crazy. He was—he insisted a hundred times—worth at least twenty-five dollars.

Frankly, King Arthur as a slave had as much value as an extra tail—that was, zero. Every buyer who considered purchasing him noticed that right away. They saw his regal posture, the confidence in his eyes, and they said, "He looketh to be a heap of trouble."

The slave dealer, of course, saw that the king wasn't exactly attracting customers like a prize poodle in a pet-shop window. So he decided to beat the king into a more slavelike shape. My fur still stands on end when I think of the whip lashes, punches, and kicks that King Arthur was given. By the end of a week, his royal body was a mess—covered with bruises, cuts, and awful swellings. His dignity, however, suffered not a bit. The slave dealer finally realized he couldn't change his slave. He left the king alone most of the time.

We spent the next three weeks walking slowly from one town market to another. I suffered from blistered paws, flea-infested fur, and—worst of all—an empty stomach. The memory of Camelot's warm biscuits made my mouth water.

The other slaves suffered much more. They caught

terrible sicknesses; several died. Four were killed by an early snowstorm. The dealer sold three others.

For a while I feared getting sold and thus separated from the king. Our terrible adventure had created a deep friendship between us. I didn't believe he would escape alive without my help. Luckily, the dealer set my price too high—twenty-two dollars. Even I knew I wasn't worth a penny over twenty-one.

We eventually reached London. I hoped that at last I could try my escape plan. I had worked out a hunky-dory scheme. In the large town, I'd be able to find a metal pin or piece of wire to use as a lock-pick. In the middle of the night, I'd undo my chains and the king's. We would overpower and tie up the slave dealer. The king would switch clothes with him. Then we'd bind him to the other slaves. The king and I would lead the slaves back to Camelot. There the royal court would recognize us as King Arthur and The Boss. We would free the slaves and force the slave dealer to get an honest job.

I described my plan to the king while our sad procession shuffled along London's filthy alleyways. I explained that we could not simply run away; the slave dealer would have every law officer in England hunting for us.

"Forsooth, 'tis most brilliant a plan!" the king whispered.

My tail wagged. The particular sound of the word *brilliant* always triggered the wag response.

London hadn't changed since my visit two years earlier: paw-deep mud, thatch-roofed huts sitting in the shadows of some very fine homes, crowds of people—some in rags, some in silk and feathers. Then, turning a corner, I caught sight of something new in the distance. Only I would have noticed it. Only I knew its importance. It made my heart sing and my hide shiver with joy. It was strung from rooftop to rooftop. Oh, messenger of progress! Oh, queen of communication! *A telephone wire!*

Bravo for Sandy and Clarence! I thought. They had managed to extend our secret telephone system. They must have been working hard that past month!

We turned into another alleyway that led to a large, noisy market square. The slave dealer pushed us through the crowd. He ordered us to sit on the ground near the center of the square. A dozen possible buyers inspected us carefully. They asked to see our legs. They checked the insides of our mouths. They poked our shoulders. One wanted a kitchen slave. Another wanted a field slave. Still another wanted an all-purpose house slave.

A tall London gentleman caught my eye. He wore a velvet robe held closed by three long metal pins. One pin was positioned at perfect muzzle height. I sat up straight. I put on my best slave-for-sale look: capable, yet very obedient. The gentleman approached me.

"What is his price?" he asked the slave dealer.

"Twenty-two dollars," the dealer replied.

The gentleman sneered and turned away to show that the price was too high. As he swung around, his robe swished past my head. I snatched the pin with my teeth. Quickly and carefully, I dropped the pin to the ground and covered it with my paw.

Step one on the road to freedom, I thought. *Now comes the hard part.*

That night, the slave dealer found an old shed without windows for us slaves to sleep in. At eight o'clock, he locked us inside. We knew he'd return around midnight—as he always did—to check on us.

The king and I waited for everyone else to fall asleep. When the sound of snoring surrounded us, I went to work. Holding the pin in my teeth, I bent over my front paws. One lock fastened each cuff. Under normal conditions, a trained mechanic could pick a poorly made sixth-century lock in a minute. However, I was working in the dark. Also, I had to move slowly; I didn't want to rattle my chains and awaken anyone. On top of all that, the king was leaning over me in his excitement, and getting in my way.

I unlocked the first cuff. I had three more of my own to unlock; then there were the king's four. After that, we would hide behind the door. When the slave dealer opened it and stepped inside, we would jump him.

The second lock sprang open. I pulled off that cuff. Then I turned my attention to my back paws.

"Be quick!" the king whispered.

I kept my teeth clenched around the metal pin. My mind was totally focused on my job. The third lock was covered with rust. At last, it popped open.

I took a deep breath. I heard footsteps in the distance. I bent over my fourth cuff. I inserted the pin into the lock. I turned it carefully. The footsteps were coming closer. I concentrated on the lock. The footsteps were moving along the side of the shed. I recognized them.

The slave dealer!

"Someone's coming!" the king whispered.

I pushed the pin harder. I heard the slave dealer unlock the door. It swung open. The dealer stepped inside, holding a tiny oil lamp. He had returned early. Our plan was ruined. He would catch me in the act of breaking out of my chains.

The fourth lock popped open. I could smell the king close to me. We both knew I had only one choice—to get out of the shed while the door was open. The slave dealer's lamp cast almost no light beyond the distance of his own hand. With a little bit of luck, he wouldn't notice me.

"I'll be back for you," I whispered to King Arthur.

My four paws carried me quickly around sleeping, bound bodies. I avoided the tangled chains. I headed for the deep shadows near the wall. The dealer moved among the slaves. He checked to see that everyone was there and securely locked in their irons. I crept forward, toward the doorway. My eyes shot back and forth—from dealer to doorway.

The slave dealer stepped around one large sleeping body. He stood between me and the doorway. I froze. I was trapped. I held my breath.

Someone groaned and cried out. It was King Arthur. He was trying to distract the dealer. His quick thinking saved me. The dealer moved toward the noise. I sprang for the doorway—and leaped through it.

Without the slightest pause, I ran down an alley that led away from the shed. I ran as fast as I could in the darkness. My muscles throbbed from lack of exercise. My paws burned where the iron cuffs had scraped through fur, down to raw hide.

My mind raced as fast as my four legs. *The king is in terrible danger. The slave dealer will discover that the highest-priced slave—me—is gone. He'll go crazy with anger. He's got a brutal temper. He'll take it out on the king because we're friends. The king is worth almost nothing as slave property. The slave dealer might kill him!*

I needed help. But who could I turn to? Where?

How? Then the answer came to me: London's secret telephone office.

I had no idea where it was located. I knew that if Sandy had set up telephone wires, then she must also have set up an office. But where? I headed in what I hoped was the direction of the telephone wire I'd seen earlier. I would find a safe hiding place nearby. In the first light before dawn, I would trace the wire to its end point.

About fifteen minutes later, I found a chicken coop that was no longer in use. It gave off a most foul odor, but I backed myself into it. With the tip of my muzzle near the opening, I waited for the night's darkness to turn to light. I spent the long hours worrying about King Arthur. I couldn't stand the idea of the slave dealer beating my friend to death. I also knew that if Arthur died, England would crumble into nothing but warring tribes.

As soon as there was enough light, I could see the roofs of the houses. I left my hiding place. A few minutes later, I found the telephone wire. I followed it along narrow alleyways all the way to the edge of town. I saw that the wire entered a small second-floor window above a butcher shop.

I paused to sniff the air around the shop. A question popped into my mind: Could the butcher make a decent roast-beef sandwich on a hard roll?

I brushed the thought aside and climbed up an uneven wooden staircase hidden behind the shop. I pushed open the door at the top of the steps and looked inside. I saw a small room furnished with a table and chair. On the table sat the telephone equipment. An object of beauty! A sight for sore eyes! On the chair sat a young fellow who looked familiar. He was sound asleep. I noticed a nicely lettered sign on the table:

Forsooth-A-Phone, Inc.

It was Sandy's work. I approved.

I tapped on the table with one front paw. The young fellow awoke with a start.

"Wha—— Stop! No one may enter here!" he exclaimed. "You must leave at once."

"I'm The Boss," I said, "and I'm in a big hurry because of a big problem. I've got to use the phone."

The young fellow threw himself over the equipment as if to protect it with his life. He reached for a dagger tucked under his belt. He took his job seriously. I approved of that, too.

"Hold it a minute," I said. "Didn't I run into you around Camelot a few times? Weren't you one of Clarence's helpers on the sewing-machine invention project?"

The fellow's mouth dropped open. He stared at me hard. "Me thinks I do recognize . . . your ears," he said. "Yet the rest of you doth appear most unpleasant to look at."

"You wouldn't treat a dog the way I've been treated for the last month," I said. "Right now, King Arthur's life is in great danger. So get me Clarence on the phone—pronto!"

The fellow got down to business immediately. He cranked up the telephone and got the Camelot operator on the line.

"London calling. This is William," he said into the voice transmitter. "The Boss is here. He needs to talk to Clarence—pronto!"

101

While we waited for Clarence to come to the phone, William offered me his chair. I jumped onto it. I put my muzzle close to the voice transmitter and pressed the receiver piece under the flap of my ear. A minute later, I heard a clatter, a tap, and then—

"Boss! It's me—Clarence. We were starting to worry about you."

The sound of Clarence's voice on the telephone—its familiar warmth and loyalty—brought tears to my eyes. I swallowed hard before I answered.

"Clarence," I said, "there's no time for chitchat. Just listen. King Arthur has been sold into slavery. His life hangs by a thread. Send five hundred fully armed knights, with Sir Launcelot in the lead. Have them enter London by the town's southwest gate. I'll meet them there."

Clarence's answer was quick. "They'll be on their way in a half-hour. Fare-thee-well, Boss."

I put down the receiver and hopped off the chair. I tried quickly to figure out a few things. The church bells had just chimed the hour—it was seven o'clock. Horses carrying knights in full armor couldn't travel very fast. The roads weren't muddy at the moment, but they weren't in great shape, either. The cobblestoned part of the road near town was badly broken, and out farther in the countryside, the road was full of ditches and ridges made by farm animals and the carts they pulled.

"At the very earliest," I murmured to myself, "the knights will arrive at three o'clock this afternoon. They'll get here later if they run into any problems on the way."

I turned to William. "May I borrow a couple of dollars, my boy? I'll pay you back when the knights arrive."

William gave me his coin purse and everything in it. I thanked him and hurried out of the building. I found a used-clothing dealer nearby. He was selling items from his rickety cart. I bought myself a carpenter's outfit to wear as a disguise. Before I put it on, I brushed my fur as best I could. After all, I didn't want to forget about my campaign for cleanliness, even under these desperate conditions.

After I ate a quick breakfast, I made my way back to the shed where the slaves were being held. It was a risky move, but I couldn't stand not knowing what had happened to the king.

I'll keep my muzzle low and sniff out the situation from a safe distance, I told myself.

I reached the alleyway that led to the shed. I immediately smelled serious trouble in the air. My heart began to pound. Dozens of people were crowding around the shed. I saw several sheriffs and soldiers. I needed to get a better view. I moved forward by squeezing between people's legs and stepping lightly over their feet, so as not to attract attention. I saw the shed door swing open. Four men staggered out. They carried something large and flat, made of rough wood.

I gasped. My four legs shook. I almost lost my balance and fell over.

They were carrying a coffin!

I stumbled to the side of the alleyway and leaned against a wall to steady myself. Was the king dead? My worst fears had come true.

My mind went numb. Minutes passed, and I neither saw nor heard anything else. When I finally looked around, the crowd had thinned out. The sheriffs and soldiers had left the alleyway with the coffin. I noticed a poor beggar sitting not far from me, leaning against the wall. I moved closer to him.

"What happened in that shed?" I asked in a low voice.

"Slave revolt," the man replied. "A very strange one, too. The slave dealer found that his most valuable slave had escaped—by magic! No cuffs broken, no chains smashed. In his anger, the dealer beat the fifteen other slaves without mercy. So they rose up against him. Together they killed him."

I could not have been more shocked if the sky had opened up and rained down snarling cats. A slave revolt! The punishment for such a crime was death. I tried to get my paws to stop shaking. I tried to make my voice sound normal. I needed more information.

"The trial will go badly for the slaves," I said.

"*Will* go badly? Ha!" the beggar answered. "'Tis over and done. It took less than ten minutes to condemn all fifteen to death. They'll hang from the gallows as soon as the escaped slave is captured."

Hang from the gallows! Capture the escaped slave! I had trouble breathing. I felt a terrible pressure—like a noose—around my neck. I couldn't keep from rubbing the fur there.

Don't panic, Hank, I told myself. *Find a good hiding place near the southwest gate. Wait there until the knights arrive.*

I took a few deep breaths, pulled my hat down farther over my head, and started to walk casually up the alleyway. I paused about ten yards before the corner. Which way next—right or left? Left. Keeping my head down, I started a slow trot, trying to look as normal as possible. I turned the corner.

"There he is!" someone shouted. "I'd know that face anywhere!"

Two men—a slave and a soldier—stood ten yards in front of me. The slave was pointing at me. I whirled around and started to race in the opposite direction. I heard their shouting and rapid footsteps just behind me. I charged around another corner. *Wham!* I ran smack into two sheriffs. My number was up.

In a matter of seconds, the sheriffs had me cuffed in irons. Then they pulled me and the other slave along the alleyways and through the public squares of London. People yelled insults at us and shook their fists.

I was desperate. If only that slave hadn't pointed me out!

"Why did you betray me?" I asked in a whisper.

The slave snorted angrily. "Let you escape! Why? You are the cause of the rest of us hanging!"

True enough. I sighed deeply. Only one hope remained—Clarence and the army of knights. They could arrive in London by three o'clock if their journey went well.

I turned to one sheriff. "When will the executions take place?"

He glared at me. "Today—at noon."

My heart sank. My tail drooped. I smelled a strange odor on my fur: hopelessness. I told myself the simple truth: *We will die hours before the knights arrive.*

Shortly before noon, we sixteen condemned prisoners were marched in one single, bound line onto a platform just outside London's southwest gate. King Arthur

105

and I stood side by side. Just a few feet from us rose the gallows—two tall posts connected by a crossbeam. The rope that would wrap around our necks hung from the crossbeam.

Several thousand people had gathered to watch the spectacle. Public hangings usually turned into social occasions. Many people even brought picnic lunches. The nobles sat comfortably in a fancy viewing stand. The common folk either sat on the ground or stood. I smelled the frenzy of the crowd. They couldn't wait for the show to begin.

The guards removed all our chains and cuffs. A priest stepped forward and said a prayer for our souls. The guards looked us over, deciding who would feel the rope tighten around his neck first. They pointed to the king.

The king stepped forward. He wore only tattered rags. His face was bruised and swollen. He had completely lost the look of his former royal self. He raised his arms and called out in his deep voice, "I am Arthur, King of England! I denounce for treason—"

It seemed as if the entire crowd of spectators roared with laughter. They hooted and whistled. "His Majesty, King of Rags!" they shouted. "Speak to us, Your Scruffiness!"

The insults silenced the king. He stared at the crowd with dignity. He was—as kings went—certainly first-rate. A guard tried to tie a blindfold around his head to cover his eyes. The king pushed him away.

Do something, Hank! I thought. *No matter how useless—just do something!*

I couldn't move. My legs felt paralyzed. My muzzle felt frozen. I was powerless.

The guards started to lead the king to the hang-

man's noose. He shook them off and walked alone. The hangman lifted the rope. He slipped the noose around King Arthur's neck.

I closed my eyes. When I opened them an instant later, I leaped forward—without thinking. I sprang at the hangman, snarling as I made my attack. Five guards tackled me at once. They grabbed my fur. They pinned down my legs. I twisted like a wild beast. My head whipped around. I saw the king, the gallows, the crowd, and the nearby hills surrounding the town.

Suddenly I howled. I howled once, twice, three times—completely unexpected howls, howls of shock . . . relief . . . joy!

Over the top of the hills, riding at full speed, came Clarence, Sir Launcelot, and five hundred knights—*on bicycles!*

Three cheers for modern inventions!

Back in Oakdale, Joe and David are about to show off their own high-tech creation—a newsletter to top all newsletters.

Chapter Eleven

"Get your copy of *The Champ!* A new sports newsletter!"

"Extra! Extra! Read all about sports at Sequoyah Middle School!"

On Monday morning, Joe and David stood out front on the school steps. They passed out copies of *The Champ* to everyone who entered the building. Wishbone stood near the door, holding a copy between his teeth.

"Extra! Extra! Weed aw-a-baw-did! Ex——"

An eighth-grade girl took the newsletter out of Wishbone's mouth. She began to read it.

"*Blech!* What a relief! It sure is difficult to speak with something in your mouth," Wishbone said. "Joe and David should use a better-quality paper. That stuff is definitely not something I could sink my teeth into! Anyway, I never wanted to be in sales. I'm more the editorial type."

The eighth-grader glanced up from the newsletter. "Did you see this?" she asked her girlfriend. "It's really neat."

Her friend nodded. "I was reading it a few minutes ago. It's great. Who did it?"

Wishbone barked. "Uh . . . excuse me. Meet the managing editor—more or less. Well, it's still unofficial."

"David Barnes and I put it together," Joe told the girls.

A crowd of students gathered around Joe and David. The two friends handed out copies of *The Champ* as fast as they could. The more comments they heard, the happier they felt.

"Terrific cartoon—really funny!"

"Cool article on football."

"Hey! I'm in the hockey-game photo!"

Wishbone noticed a red-haired boy studying the newsletter. *Oops! It's Ryan Clark, one of the editors of* Sports Report. *There's Anna Valdez just behind him. Hmm . . . do they look pleased? Make that a definite no.*

Ryan and Anna walked up to Joe and David.

"You've done a nice job on this," Ryan said. "One of you must have a really great desktop-publishing program."

"I do," David said.

"Lucky you," Anna said. She wasn't smiling. "Are you going to publish *The Champ* every week? That's what we've been doing with *Sports Report*. It's a lot of work to put it out so often. But we think it's important."

"Of course," Ryan added, "we don't have to bother to publish our newsletter anymore if you guys are going to put out *The Champ* on a regular schedule. We can't compete with it."

Joe looked at David. "I guess . . . We haven't even talked about that."

Anna shrugged. "Maybe you haven't decided yet whether you want to take over the newsletter project completely. Maybe you just wanted to show up some eighth-graders."

"But—"

The school bell rang just as David started to speak. Anna and Ryan turned away without saying another word. They entered the building. Everyone else followed them. The heavy double doors slammed shut.

Ouch! My radar is picking up bruised feelings and stepped-on toes. Anna and Ryan know *The Champ* is a major improvement over *Sports Report*. That still doesn't make them happy about the change and the competition.

Meanwhile, in sixth-century England, the bicycles cause a huge commotion when five hundred of them whiz through the gates of London.

Chapter Twelve

What a sight! Thousands of metal spokes gleamed in the noonday sun as the bicycle wheels turned round and round. The feathers on the knights' helmets danced in the wind.

"For Arthur!" the knights shouted. "For our king!"

The crowds, amazed, moved aside and opened up a path for the knights. The knights rode up to the platform on which the gallows stood. They jumped off their bikes. A moment later, they swarmed over the platform.

King Arthur pulled the noose from around his neck. He turned to face the audience in the viewing stand. Half the people sank to their knees and bowed before the king. The rest screamed and ran away. The hangman cried in fear. One of the guards tried to kiss my paws as a sign of his obedience. I told him to knock it off.

After the spectacular rescue, the king and I spent the night at his London palace. His Majesty invited the released slaves to come along, too. Clarence and I had a dandy reunion. Whenever I thought about those bicycles, my tail wagged like crazy.

Clarence winked at me. "Nice bit of work, eh, Boss? The guys have been practicing on their bikes for a couple of weeks. The rescue gave them a great chance to show off their stuff."

I thought I couldn't feel happier than I did at that moment. Yet King Arthur surprised me with something else. He stopped me in the hallway as I was going to my bedroom. He bent down and put a hand on my furred shoulder.

"Sir Boss," he said, "you asked me long ago why I allowed slavery. I told you it was part of the natural order of the universe. I know differently now. I will be the king who puts an end to slavery in England."

He turned and walked down the hallway before I could say a word. For the second time that day, a tear ran down the side of my muzzle.

Shortly after our whole group arrived back at Camelot, life there quickly returned to normal. Busy paws are happy paws, and I was busy. We had dozens of great projects going. Sandy continued to expand Forsooth-A-Phone, Inc. She also oversaw the cloth industry and the money system. After his bicycle triumph, Clarence felt ready to tackle a railroad system. I turned my attention to the newspaper business.

"You can't have a democratic society without a free press," I would say.

"Me knoweth this to be true and good," Sandy would reply. "Therefore, Sir Boss, ye needeth not repeat it a thousand times."

One morning in April, Clarence walked into my

castle office with a copy of the latest issue of the *Camelot Chronicle*. We'd brought William from the London telephone office to be editor-in-chief.

"Take a look at this, Boss," Clarence said. He tossed the newspaper onto my desk. He wasn't smiling.

I read over the headlines. I put my muzzle down on the desk. I covered my eyes with my paws and groaned.

SIR SAGRAMORE RETURNS
"PREPARE TO JOUST, SIR BOSS!" HE SAYS.
KING ARTHUR CONFIRMS DATE
SIR SAG. VS. THE BOSS: TWO WEEKS FROM TODAY

I couldn't postpone or cancel the joust. So I dropped all my other activities and quickly prepared for the big event. I realized that it was a chance of a lifetime for many reasons.

First, everyone felt the joust was much more than just a dogfight between Sir Sagramore and The Boss. It was a contest between the two greatest magicians. Merlin was working for Sir Sagramore. According to the *Chronicle*'s gossip column, Merlin had cast a spell on his favorite knight's armor to make it untouchable.

Second, knights and noble ladies were arriving from all over England to witness the big showdown. We expected a crowd of forty thousand.

Third, Sir Sagramore—a true brute—insisted that we fight until one of us died.

Fourth, King Arthur announced that we could use any weapons we wanted.

I thought over all of these facts and came to my conclusion: I would use this joust to put an end to all knighthood—not just Sir Sagramore. After that, I could introduce progress and democracy more quickly.

Two weeks flew by. On the big day, I was ready to give England the greatest show it had ever seen. I had even come up with a way to defeat Sir Sagramore without hurting much more than his overblown pride.

The joust began under a sunny mid-morning sky. A record crowd filled the viewing stands: forty-two thousand fans. At one end of the list, Sir Sagramore had set up ten large red-and-white-striped tents to house all his servants and gear. At the other end of the list, I had one small white tent where Clarence, Sandy, and I made final preparations for the match.

The bugles sounded the first call. That meant Sir Sagramore and I would exit our tents.

Both Clarence and Sandy shook my paw.

Clarence said with true excitement, "May you breaketh your legs, Sir Boss!"

I knew he meant "Break a leg!"—a theater expression for "good luck." I appreciated his effort.

Sir Sagramore appeared first. A great cheer went up from the huge crowd. He looked magnificent—a tower of iron armor on a huge horse. He carried the longest spear I'd ever seen.

I appeared next. I wore a half-gallon hat, vest, plaid shirt, and blue jeans. My horse—a sleek brown filly—wore nothing but an American western-style saddle. I had draped a rope lasso over the saddle horn.

I exited my tent humming my favorite cowboy song, "Git Along Little Dogies." I loved those old songs.

The crowd greeted me with stunned silence. I heard a few rude laughs. I paid no attention to them. From our opposite ends of the list, Sir Sagramore and I bowed our heads to King Arthur. He was sitting in his royal chair at front row center of the main viewing stand. The bugles sounded again. Queen Guenever, at her husband's side, lifted her arm and dropped her white-satin hanky.

Sir Sagramore flipped down his visor with a loud *clank!* His horse stamped the ground. The pair charged toward me at top speed. I moved my horse forward slowly. I had one end of my lasso tied tightly around the saddle horn. I started to swing the rest of the long looped rope in big circles over my head.

Sir Sagramore came within twenty feet of me. *Whoosh!* I flung the rope loop through the air. It landed in a neat circle around Sir Sag's neck. I turned my horse quickly to the side. With a loud snap, the rope pulled tight. My well-trained animal didn't move an inch. The rope yanked Sir Sagramore right off his horse.

I whooped at the top of my lungs. "Yippee-aye-ay!"

The crowd jumped up and applauded me.

Sir Sagramore's servants ran to help their master. First, they freed him of the lasso. Then they half-carried, half-dragged him back to his tent like a heap of scrap metal.

I gathered up my lasso and started to swing it over my head again.

"Who's next?" I shouted. "I'll take on any knight if he wants to challenge me!"

A hundred knights lined up on their high horses. One at a time, they charged. They knew I was challenging their whole way of life.

Whoosh! Snap! Crash! Whoosh! Snap! Crash! I yanked seven knights off their horses, one right after the other. The crowd went wild. I was in hound heaven.

The remaining knights held a quick powwow. They

116

were desperate. They decided to send out their very best—Sir Launcelot. His nickname was "The Invincible," which meant someone who could not be defeated—*ever,* under any situation.

This strongest, fastest, and bravest of all knights charged straight for my lasso. *Whoosh! Snap! Crash!* The Invincible lay on the ground like a beached iron whale. Gallant as always, Sir Launcelot raised one hand to show his respect for me. The crowd cheered like mad.

I thought the whole contest had ended. No other knight would challenge me after Launcelot. I towed Sir Launcelot carefully to the viewing stand. I coiled up my lasso and hung it over my saddle horn. I waited for the king to declare me the winner.

However, to my amazement, the bugles sounded to announce yet another challenger. My head spun around. I looked toward the far end of the list. All forty-two thousand heads in the viewing stands did exactly the same thing.

Once more, Sir Sagramore came out of his tent and got on his horse. He didn't hold a spear this time. He held a huge gleaming sword. He rode slowly toward me. I guessed he might try to slash my lasso this time. Then he would slash my head off. I knew he meant to kill me before our joust ended.

"Sir Boss!" someone shouted. "Looketh yonder!"

It was Sandy who called to me. She pointed to Merlin. He was slinking away from my horse like a low-down bobcat. He was stuffing something under his robe. It was . . . my lasso!

Before I could even move my muzzle, Sir Sagramore rode up to me.

"I challenged you to fight to the death!" he snarled

at me. "Will you keep our agreement? Or do you back down like a coward?"

Coward! My fur bristled all along my spine. I told myself to calm down. I had never before faced such a difficult situation. I had chosen a lasso as my weapon so I wouldn't harm—let alone kill—anyone. Now I had to kill Sir Sagramore, or be killed by him. I had no choice. The brute was willing to kill me as I was—unarmed and untrained for his kind of fighting.

"Sir Boss's rope weapon has vanished," King Arthur said. "He must first get another weapon."

"He shall have my sword!" Sir Launcelot said. "Sir Boss is as brave as any knight I have ever known."

You can bet I was plenty flattered. I raised my paw in a salute to Sir Launcelot. "I am most honored, gallant knight," I said. "But I always fight with my own weapons."

Clarence stepped up to me with a leather holster. Each pocket of the holster held a specially designed six-shooter gun. Clarence strapped the holster around my belly.

Sir Sagramore and I wasted no time. Each of us rode to his end of the list. We sat on our horses, staring at each other. An eerie hush fell over the crowd.

At last, the white handkerchief dropped. Sir Sagramore charged. He swung his sword back and forth, making wide, deadly slashes. I sat as still as a bronze statue of Lassie.

The crowd began to scream. "Flee, Sir Boss! If you don't defend yourself, 'tis murder!"

I waited until only fifteen feet separated my foe and me. I pressed a special lever on one of my six-shooters. The gun rotated upward. It pointed straight ahead through an opening in the holster. I pressed the lever again.

Flash! Bang! A moment later, Sir Sagramore's horse rode past me—its saddle empty. The knight lay on the ground—dead.

Servants dashed out of Sir Sagramore's tent. After looking him over, they remained speechless. They saw no crushed armor or broken chain mail to explain his death. They ignored the small hole in his breastplate. They couldn't recognize a bullet hole; they had no idea what a bullet was—or a gun.

I stared sadly at Sir Sagramore's lifeless body. I wished he hadn't insisted on fighting to the death. I hated bloodshed—especially the useless killing that happened during jousts. More than ever, I believed I had to defeat the knights and their violent way of life.

I sat tall—as tall as I could—in my saddle. In my deepest voice, I called out, "Are there any knights who do not believe I have won a complete and fair victory? If so, I challenge them to fight. Let them come at me—all at once. I challenge all members of the English knight-hood now!"

A buzz of shock and disbelief sounded from the spectators.

I raised my voice again. "You have heard my challenge. Agree to fight—or I shall declare every knight to be conquered and defeated."

The knights who stood at Sir Sagramore's end of the list got onto their horses. They did this more slowly than usual. I held my breath. A few lowered their visors. Time seemed to stop. No one moved. Then, one by one, the knights bowed their heads. They had accepted defeat.

I let out my breath slowly. King Arthur stood up.

"I proclaim Sir Boss the winner in this tournament over all the knights!" he called out.

I turned my horse and rode to my white tent. Behind me, I heard only deafening silence.

Chapter Thirteen

The morning after the joust, I awakened with a splitting headache. On the one paw, I felt sick with regret when I thought about what I'd had to do to Sir Sagramore. On the other paw, defeating the knights created the only chance to have progress, democracy, and a better life in England. I stared into my dressing-table mirror as I brushed my fur.

"Hank," I said to my image, "you must use this chance to reach your big goals. You defeated the knights, and they are the leaders of all the nobles. Your position is stronger now than it ever was before. Now is the moment to reveal all your secret projects. Now is the moment to put your permanent paw print on England." I barked at my reflection. "Go get 'em, boy!"

I met with King Arthur that afternoon. I presented a complete report on my hidden schools, mines, factories, shipyards, and workshops. The editor-in-chief of the *Camelot Chronicle* published my report the following day. I knew William wouldn't pass up the hottest news story of the millennium.

I sent copies of the report to all the major castles and large churches in England. I caught the powerful Church leaders off guard. They reacted with stone-cold silence. Everyone else was pop-eyed with amazement and mighty impressed.

I set up a business lunch with Clarence and Sandy. I wanted to discuss long-range plans. As we sat and ate our egg-salad-on-rye sandwiches—still Sandy's favorite—I delivered an all-out pep talk.

"Team," I said, "we've got to work harder and faster. Give this your best shot—and we'll win the sixth century over to every invention from locomotives to lollipops. Then we'll go for the championship trophies—freedom of religion, and democratic government!" I punched the air with one front paw and shouted, "Whaddaya say, team?"

Clarence jumped to his feet. "Now you're talkin', Boss!"

Sandy agreed completely. "Forsooth, he doth talketh!"

I had one more task to take care of right away. I knew that the knights who hadn't jousted with me might get hungry for a fight. Although I could defeat them all, I wanted no more bloodshed. To scare them off, I engraved an announcement on a thin piece of metal:

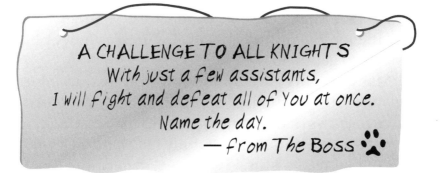

A CHALLENGE TO ALL KNIGHTS
With just a few assistants,
I will fight and defeat all of you at once.
Name the day.
— from The Boss

I hung this notice on the wall outside the castle's great hall. I also paid to have my challenge printed every day as an ad in the *Camelot Chronicle*. It worked like a charm. Not one knight stepped forward to joust. A few growled at me now and then, but most avoided rubbing me the wrong way.

Time whizzed by. I was like a hound on a hunt—fast and focused. As a result, at the end of three years, I could count almost as many changes in England as hairs on my hide.

Picture this: steamboats gliding on the Thames River; sewing machines humming in the thatch-roofed huts; elevators whizzing up and down the castle towers; electric streetlamps lighting the alleyways of Camelot. A dozen villages had their own newspapers; all of them printed photographs.

Clarence started the first of his state-of-the-art railway lines: the Camelot-to-London Express. At the end of one month, the railroad was making a nice profit. Clarence also found a way to put some troublemaking nobles to good use. He let only dukes and earls apply for jobs as train engineers and conductors. Naturally, this made the jobs seem very special. The nobles fought like alley cats to get them.

Many knights gave up jousting and instead joined in my healthy alternative sport—baseball. We had to change the rules of the game slightly to play on the long, narrow lists. As The Boss, it was only fair that I cheered in public for all teams—the Visors, the Grailers, the Moats.

Inside my furred chest, however, my heart beat fastest for the home team—the Camelot Yankees.

We set up public schools in every town. Adults as well as youngsters learned their ABCs. We started several universities. I wanted to teach a class called Shakespeare's Greatest Dogs. Unfortunately, Shakespeare wouldn't be born for almost a thousand years. I did publish the sixth century's first book—*Tickle Your Funny Bone: Dog Jokes in the Dark Ages*. My publishing company, Paws on Press, declared it a best-seller. The book was published to rave reviews.

New businesses popped up every week. So we needed a stock exchange—a place to buy and sell shares in all the growing companies. With King Arthur's approval, I located the stock exchange in the castle's great hall. The knights of the Round Table finally had a solid purpose in life—buying and selling shares. A brilliant idea—if I must say so myself. They loved to make a financial killing— much better than the *other* kind!

In the meantime, King Arthur made me happy by putting an end to slavery. Every subject in his kingdom became equal under the law. I, in turn, made King Arthur happy by telling him about my dandiest upcoming project. In his honor, I planned to discover America! I'd beat Columbus to the punch by nine hundred years!

What about the gas-bag bamboozler, Merlin? I stuck him in the local weather bureau. He was a bust at predicting the weather. He made a fool of himself at least once a day.

England was progressing and content. I was, too. Sandy and I married. We had a beautiful bouncing baby girl who looked just like Sandy. I loved them both more than life itself. As a wife and mother, Sandy was a daisy. Of course, I told her about my nineteenth-century sweetheart in Hartford. This story of lost love appealed to her poetic spirit more than I realized. When our baby girl was born, Sandy insisted on naming her Hello-Operator.

One April morning, Sir Launcelot stopped by my office to chat with Clarence and me. He asked, as always, about Hello-Operator. He was her favorite baby-sitter. I was proud to announce that my darling was crawling.

"She can get around like a comet on all fours!" I said. "I don't think we should encourage her to stand up just yet. What—"

The door swung open. Sandy rushed in. She collapsed on her knees next to me. She threw her arms around my neck, sobbing.

I gasped. "My love, what's wrong?"

The poor dear was shaking so hard she could barely speak. "H-hello-Operator! Sh-she becometh s-sick!"

"Quick! Phone the hospital!" I said to Clarence. "Send for the chief pediatrician!"

Before the words were out of my mouth, Clarence dashed to the telephone. Sandy, Sir Launcelot, and I ran to the baby's room. She lay in her crib—flushed, weak, breathing with difficulty.

I stood on my hind legs and leaned my head into the crib. I brushed my nose against my daughter's soft little cheek. Her eyes fluttered open.

"Papa," she whispered.

I pressed the side of my muzzle against her forehead. She felt feverish.

The doctor arrived a few moments later. He examined the baby gently. Sandy sat on a low stool, leaning against me. Both our hearts pounded so hard that I couldn't tell Sandy's from mine. In just the past month, little Hello-Operator had already been sick twice.

The doctor finished his exam and turned to us. "'Tis the flu yet again. Keepeth her warm. Giveth her rest and much to drink. When she is well, you must taketh her away for a month. The air rising from the valley doeth her harm. She needeth fresh sea air until she becometh strong once more."

I could never figure out why doctors—no matter what the century—always recommended sea air as a cure for so many illnesses. In the case of Hello-Operator, however, I didn't ask unimportant questions. Sea air couldn't hurt her. Maybe the change would help her regain her strength.

As soon as the baby recovered from the flu, Sandy and I packed for the trip. We had a steamship equipped with everything we needed, including a talented crew and a wonderful cook. We took the doctor along, too. I knew Clarence would keep the ball rolling at home. After all, he'd done it before. Yet I did worry about one thing: We'd have no way of getting in touch with each other at a moment's notice. Once we sailed away from England, we could be reached only by another ship. No telephone or telegraph lines had yet crossed the sea.

We spent two fine weeks cruising the English Channel, between England and France. I loved everything about sailing—my four paws skidding across the smooth surface of the deck; salt spray soaking my fur. I also enjoyed watching all the great businesses I had created. I saw steamboats with puffing smokestacks;

tall-masted ships with canvas sails. Hundreds of them rode the waves. All the boats carried raw materials and finished products between ports.

The following week, the weather turned nasty—cold and windy. The doctor suggested we go ashore in France. His great-uncle, a French duke, could put us up at his castle, about three miles inland. In the meantime, our steamship would return to England for more supplies. It would make the roundtrip in three or four days.

As soon as we settled into the chilly castle, Hello-Operator became ill again. Her fever soared. Terrible coughing shook her little body. Sandy and I completely forgot about the outside world. We thought only about our dear daughter. We cared for her ourselves, day and night. For two weeks, neither of us left her room.

At last, the baby took a turn for the better. She pulled herself out of danger. The fever passed. The coughing stopped. One morning, she held out her little arms to my wife and me and smiled.

Sandy and I looked at each other and felt the same relief, the same thankfulness. In the next moment, the same alarming thought came to both of us.

"What happened to our ship?" Sandy exclaimed.

I left the room at a fast trot. I called all of our loyal Camelot employees together. They'd been with us since the voyage had begun. Now their worried faces raised goose bumps on my hide. They had no news of the ship. For two weeks, they'd had no news at all.

I asked my host for a horse-drawn cart. With a trusted driver, I went as fast as I could to the coast. We didn't stop until we reached a hilltop overlooking the English Channel. I jumped out of the cart. I raised a paw to shade my eyes. I scanned the water all the way to the horizon. A cry of horror rose in my throat.

The sea was empty. Gone were the billowing sails. Gone were the smokestacks. Not one boat dotted the sea. My four legs shook. I shivered. Something was terribly wrong.

I returned immediately to the castle. I kept my muzzle shut tight until I was behind a closed door, alone with Sandy. Then I described what I had seen. Sandy agreed with me—something had happened in England that had put an end to all shipping activity. But what? We considered possible explanations—all of them were extremely alarming. An invasion? An earthquake? The outbreak of disease?

"There's no use trying to guess," I said.

Staring at each other, our eyes filled with fear. We knew what must come next.

"Ye needeth to return to England," whispered Sandy. "At once."

Hank and Sandy see trouble on the horizon.

Back in Oakdale, I sense the same thing after the first appearance of *The Champ*.

Chapter Fourteen

It was Monday afternoon, and classes were about to end. Wishbone napped restlessly on the grass in front of Sequoyah Middle School. He moaned. He groaned. He squirmed and batted the air with his paws.

I'm weak from hunger! I'm starving! Help me! Yes— here's my dish, filled with food. One big mouthful—Yuck! Pheh! Phooey! This tastes like paper. . . . It is paper! It's a ripped-up copy of The Champ!

Wishbone opened his eyes and sat up. He shook himself hard. *A nightmare! What does it mean? I know— never sleep on an empty stomach. But does it have even deeper meaning? Was I dreaming of a newsletter disaster? Nah, it couldn't be. Luckily I'm not superstitious.*

Just as he stood up, the school bell rang. A moment later, the double doors flew open. Students poured out of the building, laughing, talking, calling to one another.

Wishbone trotted across the grass to the cement steps. He kept his eyes on the open doors. "Joe, where are you? I want to hear the latest reviews of *The Champ*. Did we get raves? Has anyone mentioned the Pulitzer Prize for journalism? Am I up for a promotion?"

Wishbone spotted Joe. He was leaving the building with David and Sam. The dog ran forward. He wiggled between a forest of legs. He hopped over feet until he reached his friends.

"So what's the story?" Wishbone nudged Joe's leg, panting.

Joe, David, and Sam looked sad. Joe reached down and rubbed Wishbone's head. Sam murmured a cheerless "hi." Then the group walked silently to the street corner.

"Okay, so we didn't win the Pulitzer Prize," Wishbone said. That's no reason to remain silent for the rest of your lives." He barked. "Will somebody *please* say something? What's going on?"

Joe sighed. "You were right, Sam. We must have insulted Anna and Ryan by publishing *The Champ*."

David nodded. "They gave us the cold shoulder all day. So did a bunch of other eighth-graders. One eighth-grader said I couldn't be a sixth-grade hotshot because no such person exists. I don't really understand any of what's happening."

Wishbone said, "Luckily I wear a permanent fur coat. I rarely get a cold shoulder."

"Look at it from Anna and Ryan's point of view," Sam said. "You never told them about your ideas for a better sports newsletter. You didn't suggest working together. You have to admit that it looks like you wanted to show them up."

"I guess we did get carried away," David said. "We started with such a simple idea—something that wouldn't bother anyone. But then we were having so much fun. It was so easy to make all the decisions

131

ourselves. We did whatever we wanted. We got to be the bosses."

"We never even thought about producing a newsletter on a regular schedule," Joe said. "That's so much work. I guess our publishing of *The Champ* was like dumping a bucket of cold water on Ryan and Anna."

A few minutes later, the group had arrived at David's house. They were all sitting in David's bedroom, snacking on cheese and crackers. Wishbone also lapped up a dish of water. When he finished, he ran his tongue around his muzzle.

"We all feel much better now, don't we?" He looked at three gloomy faces. Three pairs of eyes stared blankly at the glowing computer screen. The masthead of *The Champ* stared back at them.

"So much for this computer victory," David said. "We'd better scrap the whole idea—including the special soccer report."

Joe made a face. "Then no one will write about the playoff game. That was the reason we started this project in the first place."

"It would feel weird to publish another issue of *The Champ* now," David said, "even a short one. I think we should just apologize to Anna and Ryan and get the whole thing over with."

"Me, too," Joe said.

David tapped a few keys on the computer keyboard. A command message appeared on the screen:

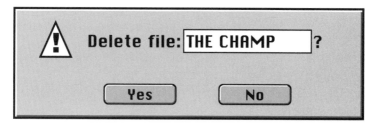

"Okay, we've decided to say good-bye to *The Champ*," David said. "One click, and this project vanishes into the cyberspace black hole."

He moved the cursor to the "yes" button.

My friends are about to make a desperate move.

Hank Morgan does the same thing when he decides to leave his family in France and return to England. He needs to find out what caused all the shipping activity to stop.

Chapter Fifteen

I sensed danger. Like a dog in the wild, my nose picked up an unfamiliar, and therefore troubling, scent. I decided to leave France secretly and travel alone. I made sure Sandy had plenty of money in case I was delayed in England. I knew that she and Hello-Operator would be safe. Our trusted employees cared deeply for them.

I crept out of the castle at midnight. My furred chest still ached from the pain of saying good-bye to my loved ones. When I turned away from them, I felt my heart would break. I wanted to capture their images in my memory.

A French sailor agreed to take me across the English Channel in his small boat. We had the moon, the stars, and the entire sea all to ourselves. I spent the night lying on my back, searching for Sirius, the Dog Star. I couldn't find it. Wrong season, I suppose.

At seven o'clock the next morning, we sighted the white cliffs of Dover, which towered over the English side of the Channel. An hour later, I set my paws on English soil.

The eerie sight of the harbor sent chills up and down my spine. I paced nervously. Dozens of docked ships sat in the water. Yet not one living creature stirred among them. Someone had stripped every sailboat of its sails.

I trotted up and down Dover's alleyways, searching for a horse to buy. The public square was empty. No merchants had their goods on display. No men or women stood chatting with friends. No children played games. I saw two or three people wandering around. One glanced at me. Her eyes were filled with terror and grief. She turned away. The silence felt like an icy wind blowing against my fur.

Hank, I thought, *there's only one thing to do. Hoof it—so to speak—to the town of Canterbury. It has a larger population, and one of England's most important churches is there. You'll get information about what is going on.*

With my muzzle pointing north, I set out on the most lonely journey of my life. For twenty-four hours, I saw no one on the road. By the time I reached the edge of Canterbury, I would have welcomed the company of a stray cat. Well . . . not quite.

It was Sunday morning. My ears should have picked up the sound of church bells. Instead, the strange silence was deathlike. On the far side of a farmer's field, I noticed a church, a graveyard, and a few people moving around. I trotted quickly in that direction. Hiding behind a tree, I watched the scene. It made my blood run cold.

I saw a small funeral procession—it looked like just some family members and a few friends. There was no priest, no holy book, no bell, no candles. The group passed by the church without entering. Everyone wept.

In that instant, I understood what had happened. I

135

looked up at the bell tower of the church for proof. There it was. The bell was covered in black cloth.

Interdict! I thought. *The Church officials have struck the most awful blow! They have put all of England under the harshest punishment.*

A Church interdict meant that everyone in England was forbidden to take part in religious services. According to Church law at the time, everyone risked eternal misery until the interdict was brought to an end.

I sank down on my belly and put my paws over my eyes. I needed to think—hard and fast. I could easily guess the cause of the interdict. The Church had declared war on my modern civilization. My absence from England had given the Church officials the perfect chance to stop the progress I had started. They were using the people's fears and superstitions to turn them against me.

I'm sure there's a price on my hide, I thought. *So I must not let anyone see neither hide nor hair of me. Riding a horse will attract too much attention. I'll disguise myself, walk to Camelot, and find Clarence. Unless . . . unless . . . Could the Church leaders have imprisoned him? Or even executed—*

The thought of my dear friend Clarence being harmed in any way made my head spin. I had to take many deep breaths to calm myself. At last I stood up, shook myself hard, and trotted back to the road. I headed in the direction of Camelot.

I bought some food and old clothes from a farmer who lived far away from everyone else. For the next three days, my four legs carried me toward Camelot. I took only brief naps, but I tried to rest my brain. I couldn't make plans until I got a complete report from Clarence— if I found him.

I reached Camelot two hours past sunset. The changes that had occurred there shook me to the bone. When I'd left England, Camelot shined like a star at night. It had more electric lights than any other town in the kingdom. Now it looked like an inky blot in the dark valley.

My civilization had been snuffed out!

The castle towered above me in the distance, large and black. I climbed the steep hill to get to it. The drawbridge over the moat was down. The great iron gates stood wide open. No guards blocked my way. I entered the courtyard. The clicking of my nails against the cobblestone pavement echoed again . . . again . . . again. I felt as though I had entered a gigantic tomb.

I stepped inside one of the buildings. *If Clarence is alive and well, where in the castle would he be?*

I headed straight for my office along unlit passageways. My office door was partly closed. With one paw, I pushed it open. A very faint yellow glow filled the room. It came from an old oil lamp sitting on my desk. Clarence sat near the desk, staring into the gloom.

I gave the door a hard shove. It closed with a click.

Clarence jumped to his feet. He rushed toward me. "Boss! Boss! It's worth everything I know to see you alive again!"

He knelt down and put his arms around me. I reached up and patted his shoulder.

"My disguise didn't fool you?" I asked.

Clarence smiled. "It's the ears, Boss. I'd know them anywhere."

A minute later, Clarence and I sat on chairs, facing each other.

"Tell me everything, my boy," I said. "And use your briefest reporting style."

Clarence gave me the news. In the past, I had always enjoyed listening to his updates. That night, I knew our world was falling apart.

"Sir Launcelot made a lot of money on the stock market," Clarence began. "He took a dozen other knights for every penny they were worth. They got angrier than alley cats—as you always say—and just as mean.

"Sir Mordred, the king's nephew, decided to get even with Launcelot. He told King Arthur that Queen Guenever loved Sir Launcelot more than she loved the king. The king turned his anger on Launcelot. He immediately put together an army. To make a long story short—"

I interrupted Clarence. "Let me guess. All the knights in England took sides—half for King Arthur, half for Sir Launcelot. The result was all-out war."

"You got it, Boss." Clarence sighed. "Battles everywhere. So many dead. I trained our first war correspondents to do eyewitness, on-the-scene reporting."

"In the meantime, who was minding the store?" I asked. "Did King Arthur leave someone in charge of the kingdom?"

Clarence nodded. "The king put Sir Mordred, his nephew, in charge until your return. But Mordred was like a snake in the grass. He declared himself to be the true king. This gave the war a new twist—it set King Arthur against Sir Mordred. They fought the final, awful battle in the southwest region of England called Cornwall. Sir Launcelot, who truly loved the king, rode to Cornwall to help him. Alas, he arrived too late."

A strong shiver shook my body. "Too late! What do you mean?"

"King Arthur ran his spear straight through the traitor Mordred," Clarence explained. "Then, with his last bit of strength, Mordred swung his sword at King Arthur's head."

My heart skipped a beat. "But the king is all right, isn't he? He was wearing a helmet."

Clarence turned his head away for a moment. When he looked back at me, he said, "The sword pierced the helmet. King Arthur is dead."

I was stunned. The noble king, my friend, the great Arthur—dead!

The muscles under my hide froze. I stared at Clarence without speaking for several minutes. His blue eyes looked different to me. Then I realized that their boyish twinkle was gone . . . gone forever.

Clarence finished his story. "Sir Launcelot has left England. Queen Guenever has become a nun. The

Church is the only true ruler now. It passed the interdict—law forbidding the practice of religion. The Church officials have waited twelve years—since you first arrived in Camelot—for a chance to crush you. They've declared that your modern inventions caused the recent war. They will not cancel the interdict while you remain alive. All England—nobles and freemen—have joined with the Church. Every surviving knight has joined in a united army. As soon as they discover that you are in England, they will attack."

My whiskers quivered with anger. "What about the scientists, mechanics, and teachers whom we trained? What about the army and navy that we put together?"

Clarence shook his head. "You thought you had rid them of fears and superstitions through education. You were wrong. The interdict scared them right back to all their old ways."

My jaw dropped open. "We have no one to support us?"

"Just fifty youngsters between the ages of fourteen and seventeen," Clarence replied. "I selected them myself. William of the *Camelot Chronicle* is one of them. They all grew up under our guidance and training. They have no fears or superstitions—they were raised with our modern style of thinking."

I sighed deeply. "We're doomed. The enemy will use all of our modern science against us. They'll take our collections of weapons, our ammunition, and our factories. They'll—"

Again Clarence shook his head. He had guessed that I would want to defend myself if I made it back to England alive. He had found my top-secret emergency plans and had prepared us for war. He had the brains and determination of a purebred terrier.

First, Clarence had set up our headquarters in a very large cave. The cave was where we had our most powerful electric generator. Wires ran from the cave to dynamite piles under every one of our factories, workshops, and weapons locations. With just the flick of a switch, we could blow up our entire civilization—everything we'd created. We could destroy it before the enemy could use it against us.

Next, Clarence prepared for the greatest battle in history. He built a long platform, ten feet off the ground, in front of the cave's entrance. Fifty floodlights were installed on the platform. Then, twelve strong wire fences were built around the cave—like twelve circles within circles. The largest wire fence was one hundred yards across. Each fence had an upper and lower wire. Each wire, in turn, was connected to the electric generator. When the electric current was turned on, any living creature that touched a wire would die instantly.

Beyond the outermost fence lay an open space that was also one hundred yards wide. It ran all around the outermost wire fence. Beyond the open space lay a ring of sand, forty feet wide. We called this the sand belt. It ran all around the open space. Clarence had buried two thousand dynamite land mines just below the surface of the sand.

Clarence finished describing the preparations for war. After he was done, I gave him a hearty slap on the back.

"Clarence," I said, "you've done quite a load of work—and you've done it perfectly. You've followed my battle plan exactly. I know just what to do now."

"So do I," Clarence said. "We will wait for the enemy to attack."

I shook my head no.

"Why not?" Clarence asked. "Our battle plan is defensive. We must wait inside our cave until the enemy attacks."

I leaped from my chair to the desktop. I stood there, tall—well, tall-ish—with my tail wagging, like a patriot holding a flag.

"Clarence," I said, "the citizens of England have a right to choose a new and better society. The king is dead. His rule over England—the monarchy—is dead, too. Now the people can choose democracy—they can govern themselves. We will announce the start of a democratic society tomorrow! Then we will defend it from our cave!"

Chapter Sixteen

Early the next morning, I wrote my proclamation— a formal announcement to all the people—of a democratic society. I had twenty of my loyal helpers get it sent all over England.

PROCLAMATION

Be it known to all: The king is dead and has left no heir. Therefore, the monarchy in England is dead. The privileges of the nobles and of the official Church have died with the monarchy. All people in England are now equal. All people can now worship as they wish. All religions are free and equal. Political power now belongs to all the people. A republic is hereby proclaimed. Every village should have an election. Everyone should vote immediately for representatives of a democratic government.

—The Boss (from the Camelot cave)

Next I sent a message to all my factories, work-shops, schools, and warehouses. I announced that every building was set with dynamite. I ordered everyone to leave the buildings immediately and not return. An explosion could take place at any time. I knew everyone would follow my order. I had a reputation for being as determined as a pit bull about such matters.

I got settled in the cave with Clarence and our fifty soldiers. It wasn't a bad setup. We had soft blankets, fresh water, and lots of snacks. I guessed we might wait a week or so for the enemy to organize its army and attack. I kept busy as usual. I had been keeping diaries for the last twelve years and now decided to turn them into a book. William did all the typing. He's a whiz typist.

I spent the rest of my time writing letters to my dear Sandy. I had no way of getting the letters to her. However, writing them made me feel close to her and to little Hello-Operator. I lay on my belly, pen in mouth, for hours. I sniffed a scarf of Sandy's and filled my mind with her scent. I imagined her bouncing the baby on her lap and laughing at my jokes. What I created in my mind was even more comforting than the precious photographs I kept near my blanket.

Several of our soldiers roamed the land as spies. The reports they brought back made my heart sink and my whiskers droop. I had believed all the ordinary citizens of England would support the new democratic society. I was wrong. As soon as the Church and nobles spoke out against the new society, the rest of the population joined them. Even former slaves sided with their owners. How horrifying! My tail didn't wag for days.

"Death to democracy!" That was the enemy's war cry. Between twenty-five thousand and thirty thousand

knights had survived the recent war. Every one of them put on armor, got on his horse, and rode out to battle with us. They came galloping down every path in England. They joined together in a single force, more massive than any seen before. The less important nobles, farmers, and tradespeople followed on foot. I couldn't ignore the truth—*all England was marching against us.*

As the army came close, I gave my soldiers a pep talk.

"Boys, you are loyal to your families, friends, and to England. And you should be! You can't stand the idea of destroying what you love. And you are right! Understand that we will battle only against the knights who raise their weapons against us. They will lead the charge. The rest of England will retreat. Over time, ordinary citizens will surely join the new society. Soldiers, you are the future of civilization. You fight for a better world! Are you ready for this battle?"

Fifty young voices shouted at once. "Yes! We are ready!"

Before dawn the next day, Clarence and I climbed the steps to the wooden platform in front of the cave's entrance. We could see nothing, but my ears pricked up. I heard the sound of military music miles away. A shiver ran down my spine to my tail. I believed completely in our cause. I refused to surrender!

"I hear them coming," I said to Clarence.

"Forsooth!" he replied. "You have crackerjack ears!"

The sky lightened. I saw a dark mass approaching slowly from the north. It looked like the broad wave of an endless sea. The sun edged its way over the horizon. I could make out horses moving at a slow trot, and I could see riders. They came nearer and nearer. Rays of sun struck the suits of armor and made them flash. I could see banners waving, plumes bobbing, and spears held upright.

When the front line of warriors was no more than a quarter of a mile from us, a trumpet sounded. The army on horseback paused for a moment, then broke into a gallop. They charged forward on the green grass that separated them from the sand belt. I watched the wide band of green grow steadily narrower under the galloping hooves. I fixed my eyes on that green band. Narrower . . . narrower . . . only a ribbon left . . . a sliver . . . gone.

Boom!!!

The land mines exploded, and the earth shook. Horses and armored knights shot up into the sky. The air was filled with sand. Splinters of metal and shreds of fabric rained down to the ground. A cloud of thick black smoke rose from what had been the sand belt. We could not see through it or above it.

I turned toward the cave entrance and signaled with my paw. The young fellow standing there signaled back to me. He flipped a large switch.

Boom!!!

An explosion shook all of England. Every piece of the modern civilization I had created blew sky-high. I sighed. It was necessary defense—but what a waste!

A half-hour later, all the smoke had cleared. The sand-belt explosion had dug a huge ditch in the ground. It ran all around our camp like a dry moat. On each side of the ditch rose a steep bank of dirt, twenty-five feet high. The banks were one hundred feet apart.

Clarence and I climbed to the top of the bank on the near side of the ditch. We guessed several thousand knights had died. The rest of the army had retreated off to safety.

I covered my eyes with my front paws. *When is war not terrible?* I asked myself. *Never. Never.*

A few minutes later, we walked back to the cave. On the way, an idea flashed in my brain. The ditch provided a new chance for defense.

"Clarence, there's a stream just south of our camp. We can change its course—make it flow toward the ditch. Then we'll dam up the waters. At the right moment, we can flood the ditch."

Clarence and I quickly created an engineering plan. The building crew—forty boys divided into two shifts—got to work. They finished the job in an amazing ten hours.

Our lookouts reported that the enemy had sent a few cows onto the grassy plain on their side of the ditch. They were testing the ground. They would grow bolder as the hours passed.

"They'll send out scouts," I said to Clarence. "Then they'll start another full-scale attack."

Clarence nodded. I pictured the attack that was to come. We'd be forced to use our electric wire fences. Many more thousands of the enemy would die. The idea made me deeply sad. My head throbbed. I rubbed the fur above my eyes with my paws.

"Such loss of life—it's a terrible pity," I murmured. "Can I prevent it?"

I got some paper and picked up a pen with my teeth. I began to write. A few minutes later, I said to Clarence, "Read this."

Clarence picked up the paper and read aloud from it:

147

"To the Honorable Commander
of the Rebel Knights:

"You fight in vain. The military strength and
ideas of our democracy are too strong. We
offer you your lives. For the sake of your families,
throw down your weapons. Surrender to the new
society, and all that has happened before will
be forgiven.

—The Boss"

"Well, what do you think?" I asked.

Clarence sighed. "Boss, let's pretend I'm the commander of the knights. You're the messenger who has brought this letter."

Clarence stood straight and tall. His face filled with disgust and anger. He tossed the paper at me.

"Tear out the kidneys of this coward!" Clarence spoke in a superior tone. "Send them back to the low-born villain who calls himself The Boss. *That* is my answer!"

My tail drooped. I knew Clarence was right. The knights would never surrender obediently. I ripped up my letter.

Night fell. I went over the battle plan one last time with my soldiers. The boys on guard duty went to their posts. I ordered all the others to get some rest. Clarence and I would watch for signs of enemy movement. I turned off the electric current in all of the wire fences.

Silently, we crossed those twelve circular barricades. I could trot beneath the low wires. Clarence stepped over them and ducked under the higher ones.

148

We felt our way across the open stretch of land between the last wire fence and the ditch's steep bank. We slithered up the dirt dune on our bellies. Or, rather, I slithered with my four strong paws and perfectly adapted legs. Clarence scrabbled along behind me.

The darkness hung like a black-velvet curtain in front of our eyes. We would have to rely on my ears to warn us of approaching enemy forces. We lay perfectly still for several hours.

Long past midnight, I heard the first sounds—a slow muffled creaking of metal.

"Knights in armor are climbing up the far side of the other bank," I whispered to Clarence.

I listened as they reached the top. Only the one-hundred-foot ditch separated us from them. They moved slowly, carefully, trying not to make noise. Those at the top started down the other side, heading for the ditch. They seemed to wait there.

"They're gathering in the ditch," I whispered. "I bet they'll send out a few scouts. Then they'll try a mass assault—their whole army attacking at once. Let's get ready for them."

We returned to the cave. Clarence awakened our troop. They took their positions immediately. I turned on the electric current in the second fence. All was ready. Clarence and I slipped past the first fence. We sat near the second one, which was now a deadly weapon of defense.

The minutes passed. The darkness pressed in around us. The night breeze felt cool.

During the next half-hour, the scouting knights approached the fence, one by one. One by one, they died. If a knight fell to the ground, we heard the metal crash. If a distant knight touched his sword to the fence, we saw a blue spark.

We had counted fifteen dead when my ears pricked up again. I heard a heavy, but still muffled, sound. It seemed to come from all around us. I guessed its meaning.

"Time to get back," I whispered to Clarence. "Their entire army is moving in for the attack."

Clarence and I took up our positions on the wooden platform. I stood on a table where I had a set of control buttons. For extra security, I pressed the button that turned on the current in the first fence.

My eyes stared into the night. I could make out a thick, moving mass—an army on foot, swarming forward. The second fence did its silent work. Dark forms—dead knights—piled up against it. This unmoving mass grew larger and larger. It slowly became a solid wall. A solid wall of dead knights surrounded us. I knew that the spaces between the other ten fences were filling up with living knights.

Clarence shuddered. "The silence. It creepeth me."

He meant, "It gives me the creeps." I agreed completely. The army moved forward quietly, hoping to surprise us. The electric current was so powerful that it killed the knights before they could even cry out. The hush surrounding the terrible sight was deeply upsetting.

I laid a paw on Clarence's arm. "The Church and the knights forced this dreadful war on us. They fight to hold on to their power. They are willing to fight to the death. We must defend ourselves, our ideals, and our new society. Shall I begin the final act of this tragic drama?"

Clarence's blue eyes stared sadly into mine. "Curtain up, Boss."

One front paw pressed a button on the control panel. An instant later, our fifty floodlights blazed. They turned night into day. The light revealed many thousands of knights between the third and twelfth wire fences. They froze, stunned by the dazzling light. I pressed another button. Electric current raced through all the fences. Thousands of murmurs of death added up to one horrible groan.

The rest of the army—still thousands more—was waiting to climb out of the wide ditch for a backup attack.

"Now!" I said to Clarence.

He picked up a revolver and fired into the air three times. That was the signal. An instant later, the boys in charge of the dam released the waters. They burst forth with a thundering rush. They filled the ditch, creating a river one hundred feet wide and twenty-five feet deep. Every knight drowned.

The battle had ended. We had wiped out the entire enemy army. Clarence, fifty boys, and I had created the conditions for a democratic England—or so I thought.

Oh, disloyal fortune! Oh, unfaithful fate! No more than an hour later, all had changed. It was my fault, my error. I—

No. I have no heart for writing what happened next. I will let the pen drop from my teeth. I will push these papers aside with my tired paws. Let my record of events end here.

A Postscript by Clarence

I, Clarence, must write the end of this story for The Boss. I will write the facts briefly because I am feeling weak.

Immediately after the battle, The Boss suggested that we walk onto the field. He wanted to help anyone who might be injured but not dead. He couldn't stand the idea of a survivor suffering. I told him we would be risking our lives. But The Boss never listened to anyone once he'd made up his mind. I picked up a bag of medical supplies and followed him out of the cave.

We turned off all the electric current and crawled over the frightful piles of electrocuted knights. We climbed the steep bank of the ditch. A knight clinging to the top of the dirt wall called out in pain. The Boss hurried over to him, bent down, and spoke. The knight recognized The Boss, grabbed a dagger, and stabbed him.

I shouted for help. Ten of the boys came running. We carried The Boss back to the cave. Luckily the wound wasn't too serious. We gave The Boss the best care we could, and he seemed to be healing nicely.

We sent a few boys out to gather information. They reported that the low-ranking nobles and freemen were gathering in new camps with weapons. We turned on the electric current in our fences for security. Still, we thought the worst was over.

Three days after The Boss was stabbed, several of the boys and I fell ill. By the next day, everyone was sick. The thousands of rotting bodies surrounding us are poisoning the air. We have plunged into a trap of our own making. If we leave our camp, we will have no way of defending ourselves. If we stay behind the electric fences, our dead enemies might eventually poison us.

"We have won," The Boss whispered, "and we are defeated." He shook his head sadly. "My modern technology has destroyed life, instead of improving it. I tried to change too much too quickly. Yet perhaps we have planted seeds for a better future. Perhaps people will not forget the taste of freedom and the fruits of progress. Perhaps something fine will come of our work . . . even if it is a thousand years from now."

Another day has passed. An elderly peasant woman appeared at the entrance of the cave yesterday. She must have sneaked into the camp during a moment when we had shut off the electric fences. She said all her family had gone to one of the military camps. She was starving. She offered to cook for us if we would let her eat. We felt glad to take her in. We were too weak to care for ourselves.

154

Another day has come and gone. Late last night, some strange noises awakened me. I sat up in time to see the peasant woman standing over The Boss. She was waving her arms around his head and muttering awful sounds. Then she turned and started to leave the cave.

"Stop!" I called out. "What were you doing just now?"

She shouted back at me in a voice full of spite. "I have defeated him!" She pointed to The Boss. "Yes, I have won! He sleepeth now, and he shall sleep for thirteen centuries. I am Merlin!"

The old figure bent over in uncontrolled screeching laughter. She—or, rather, he—rocked back and forth like a drunken person. He staggered out of the cave. We heard the terrible laughter go on and on. Suddenly it stopped. The old magician fell against one of our electric fences. He died instantly, his mouth still wide open.

Now The Boss sleeps like a stone. Nothing will awaken him. For once, Merlin has pulled off a decent bit of magic. Yet what a strange turn of events has occurred. Merlin has used his magic to lengthen the life of his greatest rival and enemy.

As I lie here, I imagine The Boss awakening in the nineteenth century. He will carry the best of Camelot into the future. He will make known King Arthur's nobility, Sir Launcelot's loyalty, Sandy's love, and my friendship. He came to our time with knowledge about progress and modern technology. He returns with greater wisdom, patience, and a desire for peace.

And what about the rest of us? I do believe The Boss has planted the seeds of a better future.

155

We have carried The Boss to a far corner of the deepest cavern. We don't want anyone to harm him during his long rest. As we laid our dear leader on a cushion of blankets, he murmured just these words: "Good-bye, Sandy. Hello-Operator."

Now I will place this manuscript next to him. He might want to have it published when he awakens in thirteen hundred years. I hope he does. It's a corker of a story.

Chapter Seventeen

There was complete silence in David Barnes's bedroom. Wishbone, Joe, and Sam couldn't take their eyes off the computer screen. David's fingers gripped the computer mouse. He was about to delete the file for *The Champ*.

"Wait!"

Joe's voice startled everyone.

"It seems like such a waste," he said. "Maybe there's some way to use what we've done. Maybe Anna and Ryan would like to have the file. We could ask them."

David looked doubtful. "Wouldn't that be another insult?"

Sam began to pace back and forth the length of the room. "Maybe Joe's right. Anna and Ryan might want to see how you've styled the newsletter on the computer. They liked your ideas. They might want to use some of the design elements."

Joe nodded. "David and I are going to try to talk to them tomorrow. We could take the computer disk with us. We can decide then if we should mention it."

Wishbone's tail thumped on the floor. "Sounds like a plan."

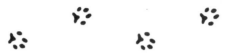

Early the next morning, Wishbone, Joe, and David walked briskly along their usual route to school.

"I'm glad you thought of calling Ryan and Anna last night," Joe said to David. "It makes sense to meet them before school starts. Maybe we can get the whole situation cleared up."

David took a deep breath. "I can't wait until this conversation is over."

Only a few wispy clouds interrupted the solid blue of the sky, but the sun hadn't yet warmed up the air.

Wishbone told himself, *This will be an honest, logical discussion among sensible individuals. Nothing to worry about.*

David glanced at his watch. "We're supposed to meet them on the school steps in less than five minutes."

The trio began to race along the side of the post office. They rounded the corner of the building. *Wham!* They ran smack into Ryan and Anna.

Everyone stopped. For a moment, no one spoke. Then four voices broke the silence all at once.

"Sorry, we—"

"Let's get—"

"I didn't think—"

"Isn't it—"

They all stopped speaking suddenly.

Joe and David glanced at each other nervously. Ryan and Anna stared at them. Joe stuck his hands into the pockets of his jacket and looked down at the sidewalk.

"Well, I guess our meeting's started," Joe said. "So . . . uh . . . David and I just wanted to say . . . I mean we made a big mistake with *The Champ*. We shouldn't have gone ahead with a new newsletter without talking to you."

David nodded. "We got carried away with all the computer possibilities. Once we started, we just kept going without thinking about anything else."

The four kids began to walk up the street together. Wishbone followed right behind them.

Anna laughed. "*The Champ* was certainly an eye-opener for us. We felt like horse-and-buggy riders who were seeing the first automobile. But after the shock, we realized we need new ideas—and help."

Ryan looked at Joe and David. "So how about it, guys? You've got talent and ideas. Do you want to work together? We'd make a sort of sixth- and eighth-grade team. That would be a novelty. You could join us for the next couple of issues and then decide if you want to continue."

Joe and David glanced at each other. They both smiled.

Wishbone jumped into the air and did a quick flip. *A merger—the joining of the two newsletters!*

"I'm in," David said.

"Me, too," Joe said. "But—"

Ryan, smiling, rolled his eyes. "But what?"

"Could David and I write about Thursday's soccer playoff?" Joe asked. "We know you and Anna will be too busy."

"I've got a better idea," Anna said. "I'll give David some help with the reporting. Joe can concentrate on winning the game." She grinned at Joe. "If you play the way you did last week, maybe we'll interview you."

Wishbone wagged his tail wildly to get Anna's

attention. "I think you also want to interview his trainer. That's me. Better yet, his trainer could write a topnotch advice column on a regular basis. His trainer would like to suggest a name for the column—'Tips from the Wishbone.'"

Wishbone's companions moved on. They were making a short detour to Beck's Grocery. Wishbone trotted behind them.

"Hey, who's in charge of hiring staff for the newsletter?" he called out. "I'd like to set up an interview."

No one noticed Wishbone. With a sigh, he slipped into the grocery store just behind Joe.

"I know I'm repeating myself—but nobody ever listens to the dog."

Wishbone breathed in the smell of pastries coming from the store's bakery department. His spirits and his appetite immediately came alive again.

"It's always tough for a dog to break into a non-traditional profession. But I'm a pioneer, a trend-setter. I'll be the first pup to break the fur barrier in journalism. As I always say, 'Where there's a Wishbone, there's a way.' Hmm . . . that would make a good title for a best-selling book."

About Mark Twain

Mark Twain was a man of many talents and many trades. During his life, he worked as a printer, newspaper reporter, riverboat pilot, miner, business-man, and internationally successful lecturer. Today we remember him as one of America's most famous and well-loved writers.

Twain, whose real name was Samuel Langhorne Clemens, was born in 1835. He grew up in Hannibal, Missouri, a busy port on the Mississippi River. Some of his most famous books—like *The Adventures of Tom Sawyer* and *The Adventures of Huckleberry Finn*—re-create the world along the Mississippi River that he knew so well. The river also inspired the name he began to use as a writer in 1863. Riverboat sailors would call out the phrase "mark twain" when they measured the depth of the river's water.

Twain quickly won great fame as a humor writer by recounting his adventures in America and his travels in Europe and the Middle East. For thirty years, his reputation and his wealth grew. He published many books during this time, including *The Prince and the Pauper*, *Life on the Mississippi*, and *A Connecticut Yankee in King Arthur's Court*.

Twain took great interest in new technology and inventions. Unfortunately, he invested all of his money in an automatic typesetting machine that eventually failed. He declared bankruptcy in 1894 and spent the next four years working hard in order to pay off his debts.

As Twain grew older, he became more discouraged about the future of the world. He criticized human beings for being ignorant, untruthful, and willing to fight terrible wars. His sadness deepened after his wife and two of his three daughters died. He continued to write, but his books acquired a harsher tone. Twain died in 1910.

About *A Connecticut Yankee in King Arthur's Court*

ark Twain spent several years working on his novel *A Connecticut Yankee in King Arthur's Court*. It was published in 1889. The idea for the book came to him after he read Sir Thomas Malory's *Le Morte d'Arthur*. This is a collection of legends, printed in 1485, about a sixth-century warrior chief named Arthur.

Twain combined some of those stories with the idea of time travel. In his imagination, he sent a man from his own time back to King Arthur's time. The result is an unforgettable tale that contains humor, adventure, and sharp satire. (A satire makes fun of the weaknesses and flaws of human beings and their societies.)

A Connecticut Yankee in King Arthur's Court has always been popular with readers and praised by thinkers. The novel has also created disagreements and confusion. On the one hand, Twain took pride in the great progress of the nineteenth century. He watched the United States change itself from an agricultural society that tolerated slavery into an industrial giant whose wage earners produced steel, railroads, and telephone systems. On the other hand, he saw new weapons of terrible destruction, poor people crowded into urban ghettos, and nations going to war for more territory and power. Twain put all his conflicting views into his novel. The result is a powerful work of fiction that makes us laugh hard and think more deeply about ourselves.

About Joanne Barkan

Joanne Barkan began to write books for young people while she was working with the Muppets. She's now a full-time writer and the author of more than one hundred children's books, including middle-grade fiction, non-fiction, titles for beginning readers, picture books, and preschool concept books. She also writes about politics and economics for adults and is a member of the editorial board for *Dissent* magazine.

Joanne read *A Connecticut Yankee in King Arthur's Court* when she about twelve years old. She never forgot the scene in which Clarence and five hundred knights suddenly appear, riding on bicycles. Just thinking about that scene would always make her laugh out loud.

Joanne loves to travel in Europe, and she has lived in Italy and France. She enjoys writing about the places she visits. She has made two trips to Lapland (in Sweden), where she saw herds of reindeer running across a valley that was about 310 miles (500 kilometers) north of the Arctic Circle.

Joanne lives on the Upper West Side of Manhattan with her husband, Jon R. Friedman, a painter and sculptor. They love city life—except during the hot, sticky summer. In order to escape the heat, they built a house and artist's studio on Cape Cod, a long, thin peninsula along the coast of Massachusetts. Joanne thinks the high dunes, wide beaches, and sandy trails of Cape Cod would make a fine setting for a future book.